# SKULL FULL OF KISSES

# SKULL FULL OF KISSES

## MICHAEL WEST

LAURA,
SOMETHING OLD, SOMETHING
NEW, AND EVERYTHING
TWISTED, JUST FOR YOU.
ENJOY!

Hydra
Publications

ISBN: 978-1-948374-27-9

Hydra Publications

Goshen, Kentucky 40026

www.hydrapublications.com

# DISAPPEARING ACT

## An Introduction by Gary A. Braunbeck

Near the end of "Dogs of War" (one of my personal favorites in this collection), there is a passage that reads:

"The creature rose suddenly on muscular legs, limp coils of rope sliding down its scaly torso. Before Ray had time to ponder how it had managed to loosen the knots, a claw blurred out, sharp talons carving bloody trails as they skated across his cheek. He fell backward, his forehead striking the edge of the kitchen table. Pain rang through his skull and the murk of the cabin was lit by sparks."

Don't worry, I'm not letting any cats out of the bag by revealing that there's a particularly nasty demon/monster in the tale (you find this out in the first sentence), but I wanted to quote that particular passage because of its clarity, its momentum, its imagery, and, most of all, its confidence; at this point, the story kicks into high gear for the type of final confrontation that, in the horror field, separates the writers from the self-deluded hobbyists – the kind of creative typist who thinks that all you need is blood and violence and a good shock or two before the final gross-out and – viola! – you've got a horror story.

The flip side of that coin is even worse: the horror writer who is embarrassed to be a horror writer because he/she believes that her/his particular gift for language and worldview of the human condition is really better suited to a more respectable genre than the one in which they currently toil, so they hide behind self-consciously "important" themes with buckets of Sturm und Drang thrown in for good measure in the hopes it will prevent anyone – including themselves – from realizing that their talents (if indeed they possess any) will never reach a more than journeyman level so long as they believe they're better than the genre they're writing for.

In both these cases (presented, admittedly, as extremes here) the one thing that makes their writing stand out is the all-too obvious need for it to be recognized as their writing, something unique to them, something that a reader can immediately recognize as a So-and-So's story within the first few lines. This need is often so intense that one gets the impression while reading said writer's work that he or she might have actually hurt themselves getting words down onto the page.

You're not going to find any of that here.

Michael West's prose never pulls a muscle trying to draw attention to itself, never once degenerates into the kind of "Look, Ma, ain't I writing good?" school of prose that is too often affected by apologists who claim they're trying to "transcend" genre – because, of course, the best way to transcend any genre is to simply *not write in it*.

Michael West *loves* being a horror writer, is in fact *proud* to call himself one, and that love of the genre, and his feeling such pride in being a part of it, is evident in each story in this splendid (and sometimes quirky – in the best sense of the word) collection.

Now this is traditionally the part of the Introduction where comparisons will be made between the author the collection and a handful of better-known writers: "...reminiscent of Stephen King," "...the next Brian Keene," "...cut from the same mold as Robert McCammon," "...the new Peter Straub," "...once arrested with John Skipp and Jack Ketchum," that sort of thing. I've always found such comparisons to be tricky at best; on the one hand, it's always flattering to some degree to have one's own work favorably compared with that of another writer whose work one has admired; on the other hand, such comparisons risk trivializing the work of the writer who has just been compared to one of the Big Names; it's almost as if you're saying (without actually saying it) that this particular writer's work doesn't possess anything to make it stand out on its own merits, so why bother killing brain cells when you can go the obvious, lazy, (and now-clichéd) route of the comparison?

But I'm going to make a comparison, nonetheless.

Michael West may very well be the Stephen Root of the next generation of horror writers.

Even from where I sit, here in Ohio, I can hear your unspoken *Huh? Who?*

Stephen Root is not – repeat, *not* – a writer. He is an actor. Specifically, he is an *extraordinary* actor (look up his resume on IMDB) who has appeared in numerous television series (*News Radio, Pushy Daisies, True Blood*), mini-series (*Stephen King's Golden Years*), voiced characters on several animated series (*King of the Hill* and *Tripping the Rift*, to name but two), and been in a staggering amount of motion pictures such as *No Country for Old Men* and – perhaps the only role people would recognize him

viii • DISAPPEARING ACT

from – *Office Space*, where he spent most of the film in pursuit of his stapler.

Stephen Root is the type of actor who is classified in Hollywood as a "character actor" – meaning that his looks do not encompass the traditional leading-man attractiveness, so he's given much more interesting and varied roles, the kind of roles that enable an actor to call upon all of his gifts and make the audience forget they're watching an actor perform a part. His is a face you've seen dozens, maybe even hundreds of times, but whose name you don't know; he's one of those "Oh, yeah – *that guy!*" actors who will be dazzling and entertaining audiences decades after the latest twenty-something hunk from the recent genre franchise of films is appearing only as a mug shot on *The Smoking Gun* after his latest arrest for DUI. And Root will prevail for one simple reason: he has that rare ability to completely *disappear* into his roles so, as I said, you forget you're watching someone act; there is an authenticity to his work that makes it look easy, if indeed you stop to consider its difficulty at all. It's Root's ability to effortlessly pull this kind of disappearing act time and again that guarantees the longevity of his career.

Go back to that passage from "Dogs of War" that I quoted at the beginning and give it a good, long look. Looks easy, doesn't it? To present something that deftly, that concisely, that clearly, must be a breeze. It isn't – trust me, I've been doing this for over twenty-mumble-mumble years and I can say from experience that not only is it not easy, it never gets any easier.

Yet because Michael West, like Root, can so effortlessly pull off that disappearing act time and again, it *looks* easy. But Michael West has far too much love for the horror genre to value anything above the story, even a desire to have a "voice" that is instantly recognizable be at the forefront. No, for him, the story is all, and if he has to disappear into the narrative in order to make the reader forget that they're reading a story that a specific writer has *written*, he's got no problems with that. And the result?

The result is the compact and terrific collection you now hold in your hands, filled with delightful, scary, sometimes funny, and always entertaining stories into which their creator has disappeared in order to give that love for and pride in the horror genre the authenticity it sometimes leaves by the wayside.

This is the Good Stuff, folks. Traditions and tropes appear throughout, yes ... but never in quite the way you think they will. It will be simple for you to not pay attention to the man behind the curtain, because these stories will make certain you never once think about who wrote them. For my money, that's as good as you can ask for.

-Gary A. Braunbeck
Lost in Ohio
July 30, 2009

*For Sara Larson, my harshest critic and greatest fan*
*Thank you for making me a better writer.*
*And for my wife, Stephanie*
*Thank you for making me a better man.*

"In the dead of night, when the moon is high, and the ill winds blow, and the banshees cry, and the moonlight casts an unearthly glow...arise my love, with tales of woe!"
—Opening incantation used to summon Indianapolis horror host Sammy Terry, 1962-1989

## JIKI

When Koji Ogawa saw the creature staring at him from across the room, he nearly dropped his end of the body. Its eyes were red, its pupils elliptical...a dragon's eyes.

"What the hell is *that*?"

"It's a *Jikininki*," Takashi told him, the cigarette he had pinched between his lips bobbing up and down as he spoke. "Come on, brother, this fucker's heavy."

Takashi and Koji shared no blood. The Yakuza was one big family.

They moved deeper into the basement, Boss Yamamoto's dead weight filling the black dufflebag between them, and Koji found that he could not take his eyes off the thing. It sat cross-legged in the center of the floor, and at first glance, had the appearance of a nude woman—golden skin; full, supple breasts; the face of a pop idol from a magazine cover-but leathery wings folded against its back, and a trio of twisted horns sprouted from its long, raven hair. Koji was tempted to believe that these monstrous aspects were just bits of costume, until he saw those wings stretch and flap.

"This is far enough." Takashi let go and the bag fell to the concrete with a soft thud. When he took the cigarette from his lips, a coughing fit took hold of him. He bent over, putting his hands on his knees until it subsided.

"You okay?" Koji asked, his fingers still clutching the canvas, keeping the back end aloft.

Takashi nodded. After a moment, he spat on the floor, then managed to stand erect, wiping the sweat from his brow with his tattooed forearm. He was ten years older than Koji, and dragging this body around had evidently been more exertion than he was accustomed to.

Satisfied, Koji's eyes returned to the creature, his disbelieving gaze shifting from its face to its wings and then back again. "What did you say this thing was?"

"It's a demon," Takashi told him, his tone oddly matter-of-fact for such a declaration. "We've been calling it Jiki." He rubbed his lower back, his lips curling into a humorless grin. "Creepy, isn't it?"

Koji shrugged, not wanting his friend to know just how unnerved he was. The demon had not blinked once since they entered the room, nor had it paid any attention to Takashi or the bag they had been carrying. And the *way* it stared at him...It was as if it had seen him before and was trying to remember where. The thought made Koji shiver a little. "What's it doing here?"

"An old priest caught it up in the Rokko Mountains." Takashi took another drag from his cigarette, his nostrils venting a long cloud of smoke toward the light bulb that hung from the ceiling. "He gave it to Boss Sokaiya, wanted to thank him for his generosity, his earthquake relief efforts."

Koji nodded. The Sokaiya-gumi was well organized. In the aftermath of last year's devastating quake, it moved more quickly than the Japanese government, providing much needed services for this ravaged community. As a result, many considered the protection monies paid and gifts given to the Yakuza well earned.

"After a funeral," Takashi went on, "the priest was standing watch over his temple when this thing came to eat the bodies."

Koji gave him his full attention. "*Eat* them?"

"That's what they do, they eat the dead." Takashi put his cigarette back between his lips and knelt down to unzip the dufflebag. Boss Yamamoto's elderly corpse slid out onto the concrete. There was a neat round bullet hole in his aged forehead, and his wrinkled face was streaked with the rust of drying blood.

The creature stood, allowing Koji to view the thicket of sable curls between its legs. He had not seen a woman naked in over a year, not since his lover Emiko...

He forced himself to look away, and his gaze fell on the sharp, black talons of its scaly feet, reminding him that this was not really a woman at all. This was a monster. He saw the thing make a move toward them and instinctively retreated a step, his eyes snapping back up to meet its face.

It was drooling.

Koji reached inside his trenchcoat for a weapon, but Takashi held up his hand.

"Don't," his friend ordered, then calmly added, "If you have a pulse, you've nothing to fear from Jiki."

While Koji was not entirely convinced there was no danger, he took his hand from his coat and returned his attention to the demon, greatly relieved to find its focus had shifted to the corpse on the floor.

"You could have sat down with Boss Sokaiya," Takashi told Yamamoto's deaf ears. "Could have shared some sake and done the right thing. Now look at you." He stood up and kicked the body in its lifeless ribs.

Koji grabbed his friend by the shoulder. "Show some respect."

"He hasn't earned it, brother." Takashi flicked his cigarette onto the floor, snuffed its flame beneath the toe of his boot, then motioned to the creature. "He's earned this."

The demon growled—a low, rolling rumble of hunger. Its mouth opened wide, as if its jaw had suddenly come unhinged, becoming a gaping maw lined with glistening fangs. With great enthusiasm, it cupped Yamamoto's head in its claws and bit into his scalp. Koji heard the crunch of splintering bone as the dead man's skull was forced open, followed by a horrid wet smacking sound.

Takashi laughed, but there was no joy in it. "Jiki loves brains," he said.

Koji stood in frozen silence, his mind trying to deny what he was seeing. His stomach rolled, but his unblinking eyes refused his silent plea to block out this desecration.

When the creature lifted its head, clumps of crimson-gray tissue slid off its chin. It spit something in Koji's direction. The object bounced off the far wall, rolled across the floor, and came to rest just centimeters from his feet.

"What the fuck was that?" Takashi wanted to know.

"The bullet," Koji told him, and then he vomited all over it.

---

"You'll go to prison for this," Emiko warned him. She was trembling, her pink scarf and jet-black hair blowing like streamers in the breeze.

"I can't marry you without a ring." Koji kissed her, then

climbed in through the jewelry store's broken window, avoiding its crystalline teeth. He found the front of the shop was three feet higher than the rear, but not by design. The quake had cracked the building in two, the rising earth lifting half the foundation on its rocky shoulders. Valuable cases lay smashed all around him, the priceless gems they once displayed now buried beneath drifts of splintered glass. He turned back to Emiko. "Give me your hand."

After a moment's hesitation, she did as he said, allowing him to help her through the opening. The hem of her skirt snagged on a jagged shard of glass, but Koji reached out and carefully freed the fabric before it ripped.

"Come on." He pulled her into the darkened showroom. "The bridal sets are this way."

She yanked his hand back. "We shouldn't be in here, Koji."

"What's wrong with you?" he wondered aloud. "I've seen you pocket candy and CDs more than once. How is this any different?"

"A pack of gum or a disc isn't worth enough yen for anyone to care, but if you steal—" She glanced back across her shoulder, as if to make certain there were no witnesses standing there, then lowered her voice. "If you steal *diamonds*, they will hunt you down."

"Emiko, take a good look at this place. In a week, or a month, it'll be torn down and the owners will start fresh. Sure, they may try to cut their losses, recover some of the jewels from this rubble, but many have fallen right into the earth. They won't find them, and they won't expect to. Insurance will just write them off and everyone will move on. Nothing we take from here is going to be missed." He tugged on her fingers. "Now, let's go."

She bowed her head, looking at the baggy white socks she

had pushed down to her ankles. "Why not wait until we can afford—"

"Do you know how many floors I would need to mop to save up for a proper diamond? It would take years, if ever!" His tone was harsher than he had intended, and Emiko cringed from it. He looked up at the split ceiling, drew in a deep breath, and said, "I'm a janitor, Emiko. I have nothing, except you. Please, just this once...let me give you something, something as precious to you as you are to me."

She sighed, and for a moment, he thought she would let go of his hand to crawl back outside. Instead, she allowed him to guide her deeper into the ruined store.

Koji brought her to the first case on the right. He pulled his hand into the sleeve of his denim jacket, using it as a mitt to sweep away jigsaw bits of glass, revealing the diamond rings beneath. One immediately caught Koji's eye. It was bright yellow gold with a huge, heart-shaped stone. He lifted it from the debris and held it up for Emiko's inspection.

"What do you think?"

"Koji..."

"You don't like it?"

"It's beautiful."

He slid it over the knuckle of her ring finger. "It's yours."

She held up her hand, watching the gem sparkle in the fading daylight from the window, and he moved away from her to look in another case.

"We should go now," Emiko urged.

Koji pulled several strands of milky pearls from a pile of glass. "What do you think of these?"

She said nothing and he assumed she liked them. He stuck them in his pocket and moved on.

"That's enough," Emiko called after him. "We should...Do you hear that?"

And he did hear it: a faint but building rumble. An after-shock. Before he could speak a word of warning, the floor shifted beneath their feet and the fractured ceiling fell inward.

---

Koji splashed cold water onto his face, as if to wash the vision from his eyes. Emiko died that day, but her memory was alive and well. Much of the time, it hid in the deep, unlit recesses of his mind, yet it was not shy and would climb unbidden into the light whenever it pleased.

He regarded his reflection in the bathroom mirror, not liking what he saw. Getting sick in front of Takashi had been the last thing Koji wanted to do tonight. It had been a sign of weakness on this job designed by Boss Sokaiya to test his resolve.

And now these thoughts of Emiko were scratching at his brain again, like a neglected pet demanding his attention.

While it seemed disrespectful to compare his lover to that demon in the cellar, Koji had seen the similarities in their figures. They were both thin, both petite, with comparable bosoms and matching hair. Take away those bizarre features—the claws, wings, and horns—and it could easily have been the exquisite body he still dreamed of saving whenever he closed his eyes.

Koji dried his face, ran his fingers through his spiky black hair, then opened the door and stepped back onto the floor of the restaurant. It was a Friday evening and the lounge was full of well-dressed businessmen who were busily chatting and throwing back drinks. In the corner, a guy stood singing *Karaoke*, his necktie wrapped around his head like a ceremonial bandana. Both his voice and his English were horrible, but his friends cheered him on just the same.

On his way to the kitchen, Koji passed several patrons eating their dinners. He wondered how much appetite they would have if they knew what was going on in the room beneath their feet.

When the head chef saw him, he bowed deeply. Boss Sokaiya owned the place, and all of his men were treated with great respect by the entire staff. It was one of the things that helped lure Koji into the life.

"Ogawa-san," the chef said to him, "I have your favorite dinner ready for you."

Koji offered a slight bow in reply, allowing the chef to stand upright again. "Thanks, Hirata, but I'm not very hungry tonight. How about some *Udon* instead?"

"Certainly." Chef Hirata gave several quick bows, as if to apologize for not anticipating the request, and turned to a member of his staff. "*Udon*, hurry!"

Koji wanted to tell them that he was in no rush to return to the basement, to the thing that waited there, but he said nothing. He kept hearing the crunching and snapping of bones; the wet ripping sounds as it ate.

Hirata thrust a carton and a pair of chopsticks at Koji. "Here you go, Ogawa-san."

They once more exchanged polite bows, and then Koji opened the basement door, slowly descending the steps into the room below. Takashi was waiting for him there, sitting at a small wooden table against the far wall, smoking another cigarette and thumbing through a stack of smuggled American porn magazines.

Above his friend's head, Koji noticed a circular design had been drawn upon the cinderblock. Inside the hoop, he could make out the characters for "heaven" and "earth," and around the outside, someone had etched a continuous stream of symbols that were alien to him. Small, lit candles were mounted on either side of the circle, and from each candle-holder hung a horse's tail of black hair.

"What's that shit?" Koji asked.

Takashi took his eyes off his porn and nodded at the symbol. "That 'shit' is what keeps Jiki here. Old magic."

"If that keeps it trapped, why do I have to stay?"

"Because..." Takashi stabbed his cigarette into a nearby ashtray and tossed the magazine back onto the stack. "...Boss Sokaiya asked you to."

"He doesn't believe in the magic?"

"He doesn't like to take any chances." Takashi stood and gave Koji a pat on the shoulder. "You did a good job tonight, brother."

"Thanks."

"Why don't I take you to Tokyo tomorrow? We can go to a bathhouse and celebrate. There are some nice girls I can intro-duce you to."

The memory of Emiko threatened to rise again, to bully him into declining, but he forced it back down into the dark-ness. She was dead. It was time he stopped acting as if he died along with her, no matter how desperately he may have wished it. "Sure, I'd like that."

Takashi flashed a genuine smile, then made his way out, closing the door behind him, sealing the room.

Koji turned to look at the demon. After its meal, it had returned to sitting cross-legged in the center of the room, its scaly hands firmly on its knees. Its mouth was now closed, restoring the appearance of femininity.

It stared at him.

"So...you don't like the taste of bullets?" Koji tried to make his voice sound as threatening as possible. He pulled a Beretta 9mm pistol from under his trenchcoat and held it up. "Behave."

The thing gave no reply.

Koji snorted and sat down. He smacked his gun on the table next to the magazines. The one Takashi had been eyeing slid from the top of the stack, opening to a photo of a blonde girl with a razor standing over a brunette with a crotch full of shaving cream. Koji glanced back at the creature, wondering what his brothers did down here all day and all night with a stack of porn on the desk and a naked demon-woman on the floor.

He winced, then flipped the magazine to the safety of the Joe Camel ad on the back cover.

*I'd give anything to be somewhere else right now.*

---

Takashi motioned for Koji to have a seat at his table. "That's a most generous offer."

"It's not an offer. It's a promise." Koji sat down. "I'll do whatever the Sokaiya-gumi asks of me."

"I'm sure you will." Takashi slid a cigarette between his lips and held the pack out to Koji.

He didn't smoke, but he took one anyway and held it between his fingers. "Your recommendation to Boss Sokaiya means a lot."

"You're a good kid." Takashi took a silver lighter from his pocket and produced a tall flame. He lit his own cigarette, and then Koji's. "You're just down on your luck. You need a chance, a way to grow. You're a janitor. Your father was a janitor. To the rest of society, that's all you're good for, cleaning up their shit."

Anger met embarrassment on Koji's reddening face.

Takashi exhaled smoke, then continued, "To the Yakuza,

however, you are what you make of yourself. You have a chance to advance, to improve your situation."

Koji gave a slight nod. "Thank you."

"Don't thank me. Make me proud to call you 'brother.'"

"I would like you to have these." Koji reached into the pocket of his jacket and brought out a handful of necklaces. He slid them across the table.

Takashi closed his fist around the pearls, and Koji tried not to show his great relief to be rid of them. "What are these?"

"I told you, I've become quite a skilled thief, an asset to the Sokaiya-gumi. This is a show of my skill and my appreciation."

"Sake!" Takashi called out.

A nearby waitress bowed and ran off to get the drink. The sharing of hot sake was the sealing of a deal in the Yakuza world. It meant a pledge of loyalty. It meant Koji was now part of the family.

Takashi offered him a warm, welcoming grin. "Now, brother, how about something to eat?"

---

Koji opened his box of *Udon* noodles. He pinched some between his chopsticks, brought them to his lips, and slurped them up.

"Why?" The tone was soft and feminine.

He turned around, expecting to see one of the waitresses from upstairs. Instead, he found the door to this basement room closed, the demon still sitting cross-legged on the floor a meter away, still staring at him, its wings folded tightly against its slender back.

The creature's lips parted and it said, "Why did you shoot him?"

He dropped his noodles and reached across the table for his handgun.

"You speak," he said.

Its red eyes focused intently upon his face. "Why did you kill Boss Yamamoto, Koji?"

His mouth went dry and his heart raced. He *had* fired the bullet this creature spat back at him. "How do you...how do you know my name?"

Jiki smiled. On a real woman, it might have been alluring. "I once asked the same question of you."

"What?"

"You don't remember?" It shook its head, but its smile never faltered. "You were walking behind me on the way to school, and you called out my name. You were a year my senior, and I wondered how you could know me. When I asked you, you said you'd been walking behind me for many months and had asked around school to find out who I was. When you learned my name...you waited several more weeks before calling it out."

It was how Koji first met Emiko. He stood and gestured with his gun. "Shut your mouth!"

Jiki looked disappointed. "Why does such a happy memory upset you?"

He took two steps toward the creature, the barrel of his gun a wagging finger. "You're a liar!"

It stared back at him, frowning. "I am what I am."

"You're a fucking monster!"

"Have you heard the story of the *Jikininki*, Koji?"

He continued to keep the thing in his sights.

"They were human men and women who were greedy in life. When they died, they were reborn as demons, damned to roam the earth with a hunger for carcasses."

"Emiko wasn't greedy," Koji roared.

"I followed you into that jewelry store, didn't I?" The creature's tone was still quiet, sweet, and calm. "I said I didn't want to be there, that I didn't want anything, but that wasn't true. I wanted it all."

He felt his stomach drop.

Jiki held up its left talon, its rosy eyes focused on the ring finger. "When you gave me that huge diamond heart, I felt like an empress. And those pearls...oh...I wanted them so badly! I wanted everything. And then, I was struck down for my sin."

Koji's hand was shaking, and the gun with it.

"You know," it went on, "the soul does not leave the body immediately. It lingers. As my body lay there, smashed beneath the debris, I could still see you."

His eyes grew wide.

"I saw you cry, heard your screams, watched you dig in the rubble to free me, even though there was no hope." Its grin suddenly withered. "And then your face was bathed in the glow of flashlights, and you ran."

A hot tear grew heavy in the corner of Koji's eye.

"You left me there...all alone," Jiki continued in its hushed voice. "If you had confessed the crime, had told them why we were there, I might not have been punished. But instead, you just ran away."

"Emiko?" Koji lowered the gun. "Is it really you?"

She nodded.

Koji fell to his knees on the hard cement floor, his lip quivering. He leaned forward, held his face in his hands, and sobbed.

"And now you're much more than a thief, aren't you?" Jiki reached out, running her talons through the short blades of his hair. "You've become a killer...a *murderer*."

He lifted his head, tears racing down his cheeks. "How did you find out about that?"

"Takashi told me," she said. "While you were upstairs he spoke to me the way a man speaks to a dog."

"I'm so sorry, Emiko." Koji rose up and took her in his arms, holding her close to him, feeling the softness of her body against his. He ran his hands up her naked back and, when he touched her wings, his sobs became desolate wails. "Forgive me, please!"

"Shhhhh." Her scaly hands stroked his back. Her breath was hot in his ear, "I'll forgive you, Koji. It's not too late. You can still make this right."

"Just tell me what to do," he begged.

———

"Shoot the bastard." It was Takashi's voice, but the order was Boss Sokaiya's.

Koji glanced at him, then returned his eyes to the elderly man behind the black lacquered desk. Boss Yamamoto. Koji's 9mm aimed at his receding hairline.

"You don't want to do this," Yamamoto pleaded.

"Sure he does." Takashi holstered his own gun and made himself comfortable in one of the office's high-backed leather chairs. The glass table in front of him displayed an elephant tusk carved into a detailed sculpture of bonsai trees and pagodas. Takashi put his shoes up on the glass, kicking the ivory to the carpet. "Unlike you, he respects the Sokaiya-gumi's wishes."

Yamamoto, this man who controlled so much, could not control his own tears. "I have a wife, a daughter. My daughter, she's...she's pregnant. In three weeks, I'll be a grandfather for the first time."

Takashi rolled his eyes. "Please, Koji, shut...him... up!"

Koji started to squeeze the trigger, sweat beading on his

forehead. He had to do this. Botching such an important task would mean facing Boss Sokaiya, would mean cutting off his own little finger to atone for his failure. And that was if Sokaiya was feeling merciful.

"Please," Yamamoto cried, looking past the barrel of the pistol, looking right at Koji. "You're not like your friend here. You've never killed anyone before."

Koji saw Emiko disappear beneath the jewelry store's collapsing roof, saw her blood carving rivers in the dust, and a tear stung his eye. "Yes, I have."

He pulled the trigger.

Yamamoto's death was different than Koji had envisioned it. The man's head did not come apart and bloom into a flower of blood. It simply jerked back, and then snapped forward again. His lifeless body fell across the desk, leaking a scarlet pool that spread outward from the epicenter of his wound, greedily consumed the papers it found there.

Takashi put his hands together in a slow clap, then reached down to unzip the dufflebag. "Let's go to work."

———

Koji ripped the black tassels from the candleholders and held them in the flames. They instantly ignited. He dropped the strands in the ashtray, watching them burn, smelling the musty stench of their smoke.

"It was my hair." Jiki touched the top of her head, a small bald spot at the root of her center horn. "That horrible priest ripped it out."

Koji took off his over-sized trenchcoat and wrapped it around her body, hiding both her wings and her nakedness. He then grabbed her by the hand and led her toward the door. "There's a car parked in the alley behind the restaurant. We walk up the stairs, out the back door, get in, and drive off to the mount—"

"What the hell are you doing?"

At the sound of Takashi's voice, Koji drew his 9mm and pushed Emiko behind him.

His friend drew two pistols of his own, holding one out in each hand as he stepped into the room. "I asked you a question, brother."

"I'm taking her out of here."

"You're taking *her* out." There was concern in Takashi's voice, but his guns remained steady. Both were aimed at Koji's chest. "That's not a woman, brother. It's a monster, a demon."

Koji nodded. "And I had a part in that. Now, put your guns down."

Takashi shook his head, his eyes shifted to the symbol on the wall for a moment, to the hairless candleholders, then snapped back. "You're about to make a horrible mistake, and I can't let you make it."

"There's no mistake," Koji assured him, keeping his aim steady. "I know her. You treat her like a pet."

"I don't know what spell that thing has you under, what promises it made you, but it lies, brother. It says what it thinks you want to hear, whatever it takes to get you to free it."

Jiki squeezed Koji's hand, whispering softly in his ear. "It's true. I've lied to your brothers, promised them things I never intended to give, anything for my freedom. Would *you* have done any less if you'd been captured — held against your will?"

Koji tightened his grip on the gun. "Takashi, you are my brother, but I will shoot you through the head if you don't get out of our way."

"It belongs to Boss Sokaiya, and I can't let it leave this room."

"Then you force me to kill you."

"Why the fuck are you doing this?"

Koji shrugged. "I love her."

"You...?" Takashi's eyebrows rose. "That *thing* eats corpses!"

"Then don't."

Spittle flew from Takashi's lips. "Drop your fucking gun!"

They fired at the exact same time.

Koji's bullet struck Takashi between the eyes and the back of his head erupted onto the doorframe. He collapsed like a marionette who's strings have been cut, his legs shaking in a death spasm.

Takashi's shells tore through Koji's chest and abdomen. He fell back into Jiki's waiting arms, his insides burning. When he held his hand up to his wounds, he felt a hot gush against his palm. He looked down at his red fingers and cried out.

Jiki lowered him to the concrete floor. "Koji?"

"I'm sorry...Emiko." He drew in breath with harsh, wet rasps, feeling razorblades in his chest. "It doesn't look like I can help you anymore."

She turned away from him, looking across the room to Takashi's body. Koji saw her nostrils flair, and then she slicked her lips with her tongue.

"Emiko...no!" He reached out with bloody fingers and grabbed for her hair. "Not brother!"

But she wasn't listening. Instinct had taken over. When she pulled away, Koji found that he was too weak to hold her back. She crawled across the floor, grabbed Takashi by the head, and pulled him toward her mouth. Koji saw his friend's glazed eyes staring back at him, saw them disappear beneath rows of glistening fangs, saw blood flow, then could watch no more.

After she had finished him, Jiki returned, lifting Koji off the cold, hard floor. "You gave him the pearls."

"The...?"

She nodded. Her chin was red and shimmering. "The ones you stole. You gave them to Takashi."

"They were...a reminder of your death, of my sin." He tried to draw in breath, but his lungs were full of fluid. He coughed some up, then touched her cheek. "Please," he gargled, "Emiko...forgive me."

She sniffed his fingers, and the corner of her mouth curled into a sly grin. "He gave them to a whore in Tokyo. She wrapped them around his cock during fellatio."

"He...?" Koji withdrew his shaking hand from her face. "How...how could you know that?"

"Takashi knew," she explained. "And when I consumed him, I knew it too. Just as I knew you pulled the trigger, because I saw it through Boss Yamamoto's eyes when I swallowed his brain. His daughter wasn't really pregnant, you know. He made it up. He really didn't think you would shoot him. But you proved him wrong, didn't you? You proved both of them wrong."

Koji felt suddenly cold.

"You...stole their memories?" he asked, and then her words from earlier replayed in his groggy mind: *The soul does not leave the body immediately. It lingers.*

Jiki said nothing. It just sat there, watching the blood drain from his wounds, waiting.

# THE BRIDGE

Kim Saunders chewed her lower lip, trying not to let this little field trip bother her. She sat in the passenger's seat, dressed as Little Red Riding Hood with a small wicker basket resting in her lap. Angela Peter's party had been totally lame. Bobbing for apples? Did she think they were all still in the fifth grade? Carter Donovan, her boyfriend, drove—his face painted like Brandon Lee's *The Crow*. He was a wide receiver on the football team, two years her senior, and incredibly gorgeous even in ghoul make-up. She would've gone anywhere he asked her to. And it wasn't like they were going alone. There were Tony and Tina, Mark and Ellen...three couples crammed into an old station wagon on a dark country road. Safety in numbers, right? There was nothing to be nervous about. Nothing. After all, there were no such things as ghosts... even on Halloween.

As Edna Collings Bridge drew nearer, she found her heart thudding louder in her ears. "Old" places bothered her. It wasn't that she found them creepy, although she did. If she spent enough time in some buildings, she got physically ill—headaches, nausea, chills. There were even older portions of the school that made her head spin. The doctor chalked it up to a simple mold allergy or mild asthma.

These breathing problems had made her mother overprotective to the point of smothering. The woman would go crazy whenever Kim got a simple bruise or scrape. More recently, they nearly came to blows over the issue of Kim's driver's license. Her Driver's Ed instructor granted her a waiver, but dear old Mom said she needed more practice. At last her father—

*The voice of reason!*

—stepped in to say she'd earned the right to take the test.

"Amy, just because she has a license doesn't mean she can take off whenever she wants," he said, then reminded her, "We still hold the car keys."

Her mother gave him that scolding glare of hers—the one that said, "You always give in to her"—but she finally agreed to let Kim take the test.

*Which I passed, thank you very much!*

And what would Mom think of this late night ride to the middle of nowhere?

*She wouldn't like it at all,* Kim thought with a smile. *Which is all the more reason to do it.*

The car entered the gaping maw of the elderly covered bridge. Faint light from the dashboard was all that stood between them and total darkness. Carter drove to the middle of the overpass and stopped.

"Turn off the motor," Mark called from the back seat, his voice filtered through the hockey mask he wore. "You gotta turn off the motor."

Carter nodded and pulled back on the key. The engine coughed several times, then died. After a moment of uneasy silence, he gave Kim a wink and she smiled in spite of her fears. Slowly, he turned to face the back seat. His letterman jacket made an odd creaking sound. "Has everyone heard the story?" he asked.

Tony pulled off his ninja hood and grabbed Tina by the shoulders. "She hasn't."

The Hershey's flag from Tina's silver kiss costume slapped him across his face. "It's bullshit, whatever it is."

"We'll see, won't we?" Carter grinned—a gothic clown with a campfire story for the kiddies. "Back in the 20's there was this family who would come here for picnics along the stream that runs right under this bridge. They would eat and lounge around, the father would fish, and the little girl would swim in the stream. When it started to get dark, the parents would drive into this covered bridge, turn off their motor, and honk three times. That was the signal for the little girl that it was time to go home.

One day, when they honked their horn, the girl didn't come. They looked everywhere for her and, finally, they found her body. She'd drowned." He paused for effect, his eyes spanning each of their faces before continuing. "They say that if you drive into this bridge at night, turn off your motor, and honk your horn three times—"

Mark cut him off, "I thought it was five times?"

"That's *Candyman*," Ellen corrected with a nervous giggle. Kim couldn't believe her mother let her walk out of the house in that dominatrix outfit.

Carter went on. "You honk your horn three times, just like her parents did. If you do that...the ghost of that drowned little girl will come get in the car, ready to go home with you."

There was another brief silence, broken by Mark's mock moaning. Ellen elbowed him and Tony laughed.

"Shut-up everyone." Carter placed his hand above the steering wheel, ready to smack the horn. "You guys ready?"

They nodded.

He hit the horn...once...twice...three times.

Kim looked around nervously. She felt something brush her leg and stiffened in her seat. Thankfully, she didn't shriek. When she looked down, she could barely make out Carter's hand in the darkness-stroking her thigh.

"How long is it supposed to take?" Tina asked.

Tony put a finger to her mouth. "Shhh! You'll scare away the ghost."

There was something coming toward them-a dark shadow blotting out the square of moonlit road on the opposite end of the bridge. Whatever it was, it had wings. Before Kim could say a word, the form collided with the windshield.

The girls screamed at the loud thud.

"What the hell was that?" Tony wanted to know.

"It was a bird," Carter told them, his hand left Kim's thigh —feeling the glass where the animal impacted. "Damn thing smacked right into us."

"It wasn't a bird," Kim told him, clutching the handle of her basket. "It was a bat."

He shrugged. "Maybe. This place is old and in the woods."

"And haunted," Mark added with a nervous giggle, puffs of breath rising like smoke signals from his lips.

"Don't bats have radar or something?" Ellen asked, then shuddered. "Start the motor again, I'm freezing."

"We can't," Tony huffed. "The ghost won't show if the car's running."

"The ghost isn't gonna show anyway," Tina assured him, "because there's no ghost."

Behind Kim's head, the passenger window shattered. An ice storm of glass blew inward, stinging the bare skin of her right arm and leg. Her hair broke free of her hood, blowing across her face like a tattered shroud. Between the strands she saw a figure step from the shadows. It moved closer to her door—a little girl with a blue, wrinkled face, sunken eyes, and green hair matted with sediment.

"I'm ready to go," the dead thing said, its voice no louder than a whisper. "Ready to go home."

It reached into the car and grabbed Kim by the arm. Its flesh was soft and horribly spongy. She screamed until she thought her throat would rupture, until the sound began to unravel into a hoarse whining. Carter turned on the engine and slammed his foot on the gas. As the car lurched forward, the little girl's wet grip slipped from Kim's wrist.

When they cleared the bridge, Kim slid across the seat, stray slivers of grass carving into her legs. She was still trying to scream as she climbed into Carter's lap. The car stopped quickly, a cloud of dust rising from the road, and he tried to find out if she was okay. For what seemed like an eternity, she couldn't speak. Finally, she told him, "It touched me! It touched my arm!"

Carter Donovan had not seen the dead girl. None of them had. They thought another bat had flown at the station wagon, thought it had brushed against Kim before retreating into the dark. She never told them what really happened. Insurance paid for new glass, Band-Aids covered the cuts she received from the broken shards, but nothing could fix her shattered sense of reality, and nothing could cure her newfound fear of the dark.

# DOGS OF WAR

This time Raymond Speck had captured one of them alive. It now sat in his kitchen, struggling against the old rope that bound it to the chair. Rivers of shadows flowed across its ashen skin as a hard rain pelted the lone window of the cabin. A fall of matted, raven hair spilled around its horns and stuck to its face-caught in the excretions that slimed its scaly flesh. The creature peered into the dimness, assessing its situation with soulless, predatory eyes. After a moment, it stopped squirming and looked Ray squarely in the face.

"Please..." the demon moaned across withered lips. Its teeth were rows of sewing needles. "Please let me go. I won't tell them where you are. I won't say anything."

Ray turned away, afraid it might hypnotize him. Afraid it might make him free it, or worse...make him hurt himself the same way another of its kind had made Denny hurt himself. That had been fourteen years ago. Had he really been on the run for fourteen years?

He wondered for a moment what would happen if the books he had been reading were just made-up bullshit, and his stomach sank. He saw the knife on the counter, saw his own nervous eyes stare back at him from its shimmering blade. It was too dangerous to keep this thing alive. He should kill it now, pack his things, and move again. But Ray had grown so tired of running. He wanted this nightmare to be over, and for that he needed some answers.

He upended the Morton Salt canister, creating a snow shower that closed the white circle he had made on the floor. When he shut his eyes and began to pray, the sound of the rain was loud in his ears. It had been raining that night too, the night this all began. Cats and dogs, his mother used to say. Yes, it had been raining cats and dogs when Denny Freeman ran into the bar...

"You've got to let me stay with you tonight." Denny had said, his lips quivering like he was about to cry. Ray had never seen a black man that pale. "He...he knows where I live, where I work. I saw him outside just now. He followed me here."

If this wild-eyed man had sat down next to anybody else in O'Shay's Tavern, they probably would have gotten up and left right then, but Ray had served with Denny in the Gulf. Before that, they'd both been weekend warriors—collecting their beer money from Uncle Sam, thoughts of fighting a real war never cropping up. Then their National Guard unit got the call and they kissed their lives good-bye for a cot and sand as far as the eye could see. When you dodge bullets with someone, you get to know who they really are, and Ray trusted Denny with his life. "What'd you see?"

Denny nodded, then looked at the mug of Bud Light on the coaster in front of Ray. "How many you had?"

"This is my first." He paused a moment, then asked the

question that had been gnawing at his lips since his friend ran in from the storm, "How many you had?"

"I ain't touched a drop." Denny's words carried no defensiveness. They were hollow, like his cheeks. "It started about a week ago, when I left here. I went down onto the subway platform and I saw something moving in the shadows. At first, I thought it was the rats. I could hear 'em back there, squeakin' and shit. The train was runnin' late and I just kept lookin' over there into the dark. After a while, I could see something else-something *big*.

"I don't know why I walked over there, but I did. I walked over to the edge of the station-where it disappears into the big tunnel-and I see him. He looked kinda like a man at first, but then I could see his fingers were too long and his nails...his nails were like claws. And his face was...he had horns."

Ray wondered what kind of horns. Why, he didn't know. What difference did it make, right? But Denny said they were long and black. He said the ends were white, like they'd been stuck in a pencil sharpener.

"That's how I knew it was the devil," Denny went on to say. "He was just sitting there, watching me. I was about to run away when he actually spoke."

"What did he say?" It was all Ray could think to ask.

Denny's eyes did not belong in his weathered, ebony face. They were eyes that should have been bulging from a six-year-old boy, alone in the dark and afraid of his open closet. "It said, 'I know you.'"

"Anyway, the train came and I ran like hell. I thought maybe I'd just had too much to drink, maybe I dreamed the whole thing, but I saw him again on my way to work. He tried to hide in an alley next to the bank, but I could still see him. You ever seen pictures of those old carnivals? The dog-faced boy? That's what this thing was. His skin was whiter than yours and his eyes...at first; I didn't think he had any eyes. They were there, though, like two black marbles shoved into his face. When I went outside at lunch, he was still there. He's been there every day this week, watching me. I think he's waiting for me to be alone.

"Tonight, I walked into my building and saw him hiding under the stairs. This cockroach ran across the floor and he reached out and grabbed it. He grabbed it and ate it. I just turned and ran. I think I ran all the way here. I'm just about to open the door when I hear this bottle rolling on the concrete and I looked up. I couldn't help it. Reflexes, y'know? Wanna guess what I saw? "

There was something moving in Ray's gut and he drowned it with the rest of my beer.

"I saw him coming at me," Denny said. "His mouth was open and I could look right down his fuckin' throat, and the smell...smelled like...smelled like death itself."

"So why you?" Ray had to ask.

"I've been thinking 'bout that," he said with hesitation. "And don't ask me why, but I keep thinking it's got something to do with the war. My grandfather used to tell me stories about marching in Alabama. He said they had these dogs trained to just maul the black folks. Couldn't have you white sons-o'-bitches getting torn apart with all those television cameras. Sadam... maybe he's got this thing trained too. Hell, with all those weapons labs out there, maybe he had some mad scientist *make* it. All I know is this thing wasn't after me before we went to war." Denny actually snickered a bit and added, "Or maybe it really is the Devil. Maybe it's the Rapture and we're all goin' to Hell."

The bartender brought another drink and Ray began nursing it. Part of him was waiting on Denny to add more to the tale, another part wanted him to say it was April Fools or

Candid Camera or something, but he didn't. He just sat there. Maybe he was waiting for Ray to tell him he was crazy in the head. They'd both heard the stories. Guys came back from the desert with all kinds of weird symptoms. Some were going blind. Some couldn't even get out of bed in the morning. Some had rare cancers and kids born... wrong. "Gulf War Syndrome" they were calling it, but no one knew what it was. They blew up those weapons dumps, all those labs, sent shit billowing up into the air, and no one knew what it would do to them. Nobody knew what they'd all been exposed to over there —what they'd brought back with them.

They sat silently watching the old Zenith at the end of the bar. The Knicks were playing. Neither of them said another word until the game was over. Then Ray told Denny he could crash at his place if he wanted to. Denny thanked him and they left the bar together, feeling the sudden cold of the wind. They walked half a block toward the subway.

Denny wasn't ready for that. Even a six-pack couldn't extinguish his fear completely. "You're not goin' down there, are you?"

"How else we gonna get home?" Ray hadn't meant to snap at him, but he'd been drunk and was starting to get one whale of a headache.

Denny blinked at him and said, "Taxi. Bus. Shit, I'll walk."

Ray stumbled down the narrow flight of stairs. In his inebriated state, it seemed as if they were rolling beneath his feet, but he kept his balance and avoided taking a header onto the tile. When he reached the first landing, he took a look around to find the station deserted, then turned back to Denny. "The coast is clear, man."

Denny looked at him as if he wanted to say something, but instead he grabbed the railing and began his own slow, deliberate descent. When he joined Ray, they staggered down to the edge of the track. Denny kept looking around nervously. Ray thought if he said "boo" the man would have vaulted free of his skin. Up to this point, he kept thinking maybe his friend was joking. He thought they'd both get a good night's sleep and laugh about everything in the morning.

Then Ray saw the creature for himself.

Something moved in the tail end of his eye. Ray's mind was trying to tell him it was nothing, but the ache in his temples beat it into believing what he was seeing. It was Denny's devil, sitting Indian style over a heating grate, watching them like some sculpted gargoyle. Ray could see its small, black eyes staring back at him from the gloom. The face around those eyes was ghostly white and the smile below them was a crocodile's grin. Its teeth glistened even in the gloom. As bad as that was, it wasn't until Ray saw the horns that he began to scream.

Denny was screaming behind him, and Ray turned just in time to see him fall across the arriving train's path. Tests would later show he was legally drunk at the time. The police questioned Ray at some length, but he didn't tell them what he'd seen, what drove Denny to run blindly into the arms of death. They were quick to rule the death an accident, and the whole affair was quickly forgotten.

But Ray couldn't forget.

After a week of sleepless nights, he went back to the early morning emptiness of that subway station. The creature was there, lurking in the shadows and the moist heat seeping up from the grates—its face armed with those sharpened bull's horns. A rat crawled across the twisted flesh of its legs and it stroked the animal with its claw as if it were a kitten. Ray pulled a butcher's knife from under his coat and buried it in the beast's pale belly. Its cries echoed through the vastness of the subway station and tunnels. Ray kept stabbing the animal until its wailing died in his ears, knowing it wouldn't bring Denny back and not caring. Whatever this beast was, it needed to be killed. He continued stabbing it until the ache in his arm and head screamed for him to stop.

The next night, another of the creatures was lying in wait in the alley beneath Ray's window. It must have heard the death cries of its twin and seen him, must have followed him home. He crept up on this new monster when it was riffling through a dumpster for filthy scraps of rotten food. He wrapped his tie around its thick, pulsating throat—tightening it until the animal stopped writhing and fell limp onto a bed of Hefty bags—and then Ray left New York.

He began to feel like *The Fugitive*. He would be on his way to starting a new life somewhere when one of these things would show up, forcing him to abandon everything in the dead of night. Along the way, he would kill as many as he could, hoping to keep them from following his every move, but it never stopped them. They were always able to pick up his scent, even in this log cabin in the middle of the wilderness.

―――――

Ray abruptly halted his prayer and opened his eyes. His head was aching. He filled a glass with clouded well water from the faucet and drank deeply, his hand and lips trembling. After a moment, he put the glass down on the counter and reached for the butcher's knife.

When the beast saw the blade, it began to whimper.

Ray ignored the sound and slowly approached his captive, hoping the salt would bind the beast to the chair even if the rope did not. Ray knew what had to be done. He would begin making slits in the tight skin of the thing's chest until it told him what he wanted—no, *needed*—to know.

The creature rose suddenly on muscular legs, limp coils of rope sliding down its scaly torso. Before Ray had time to ponder how it had managed to loosen the knots, a claw blurred out, sharp talons carving bloody trails as they skated across his cheek. He fell backward, his forehead striking the edge of the kitchen table. Pain rang through his skull and the murk of the cabin was lit by sparks.

His ring of salt did nothing to hold the creature in place. It bolted into the next room, and Ray could hear the sound of heavy chains banging against his wooden door, keeping perfect time with the throbbing of his temples. All the doors were padlocked. The only way out was with a key. Grabbing up the knife, Ray ran to the open doorframe that separated his kitchen from the rest of the cabin. With great caution, he peered around the wooden molding toward the front door.

This monster was frantic, crazed.

It pulled at the chain with its talons, trying to break the padlock with brute strength. When this failed, it began to pound on the door in frustration. The beast's tail was swinging wildly through the air, and Ray found himself watching it with more than a bit of curiosity. It ended in a point, like an arrowhead, like the Devil's tail. After a moment, the thing stopped trying to break down the door and scanned the room with its black eyes. It was making a strange mewling noise. If Ray didn't know any better, he would have said it was actually crying.

And then it saw him.

At first Ray thought it was just staring off into space, contemplating its hopeless predicament with glacial eyes. Then it charged at him in a frightening blast of acceleration, launching itself across the room with its powerful hindquarters, its five-clawed toes digging into the wooden floor like the spikes of cleated sneakers, its horns giving it the appearance of a crazed bull. Ray stumbled backward in fear, but it was on him in an instant. It wrapped its talons around his forearm and pushed him down to the floor, trying to pry the knife from his grip. Its howl was ear-splitting; filled with rage, fear, and exertion. The black hair of its mane bristled and its mouth opened to bite Ray's wrist.

The pain was incredible.

Ray wrapped his free arm around the monster's throat and strained to loosen its hold. Its mouth came away in a splash of Ray's own blood and he wasted no time in plunging the knife into its chest. There was a terrible, shrill screech from the beast and it writhed in his grip, desperate to work itself free. Ray pulled the knife out—the wound arcing blood across the scales of its chest—then stabbed it again. And he kept stabbing it. He stabbed it until the arcing blood and the yammering stopped.

When Ray was certain the monster was dead, he slid out from under its carcass and shuffled over to the kitchen sink. The cold running water washed away the blood, but the mark remained. He bandaged it tightly with a dishrag and sat down at the kitchen table. He sat there for what seemed an eternity. Normally, he would have fled out the door and out of town. But he was tired of running from them and, to be honest, he didn't think there was anywhere left to go.

Ray dragged the lifeless hulk from his cabin and threw it in the back of his Jeep. He drove for some time, looking for just the right place to bury the monster. If others of its kind could smell its corpse, he didn't want them to be at his doorstep when they found it. He went deep into the woods and dug a hole in the soft earth. He spent most of the night digging and, when he felt it was deep enough, Ray put the creature in its grave and covered it over with muck.

Six months passed before they found the creature's body. Toby Greer was out hunting, and his dog went and dug it up. Decay must have really done a number on it because everyone in town thought it was a human being, a woman. Ray couldn't believe it. How many women had a four-foot-long tail? It's amazing what the mind will come up with to protect itself from the truth. But he couldn't really blame them. He wished he was still that innocent.

A few days later, Ray saw a news crew when he went to get some Advil. A female reporter was standing on the corner so that her cameraman could get a good shot of Main Street as she spoke. "...and the victim has been identified as 22-year-old Nikki Miller. An autopsy revealed the girl had been bound with rope and may have been held captive prior to being stabbed more than thirty times."

When he walked into the drug store, Ray overheard more talk about this poor girl, heard them say she was found naked, that this was the work of some sexual pervert or serial killer.

He was about to ask someone what was going on, but the thing in the security mirror caught his eye. One of the monsters was following him, stalking him. It tried to stay hidden, but Ray could see it. He didn't react, didn't give any hint that he knew it was there, and after a moment, it retreated out the front door. Ray ran after it, going to the window, watching as the thing climbed into a car parked outside. He knew the car, too. It belonged to Fred and Mary Drake. The creatures must have killed them, must have been using their home while they searched for him.

After fourteen years, Ray wasn't going to run, wasn't going to just hide himself away up in his cabin and hope that they would let him be. He finally had the upper hand, and he was going to make the first move. He loaded some knives and a shotgun into his Jeep. Tonight, he would go and wipe out the whole fucking nest. He was going to send all of these demons straight back to Hell. Then, maybe it would finally be over. Maybe... God, his head was killing him! He took more Advil, but it didn't seem to be helping anymore.

*Jesus*, Ray thought as he gnashed his teeth together against the pain. Poor Fred and Mary.

They had four kids.

# TROLLING

Scott Jarvis was shocked when he opened the door and saw huge teeth gleaming in the light—an eight-foot-wide set of shark's jaws, mounted to the bar's back wall, surrounded by fishing nets, framed photos, and other décor—but what he saw next was even more surprising. A big-breasted woman sat on the far stool. Alone. He knew the teeth had to be fake, but he hoped those breasts were real.

There were vacancies on either side of her, but Scott chose instead to sit two stools down. Experience had shown him that sitting down right beside a woman when other seats were available only served to spook her. He had to make a gradual approach, had to make sure she didn't feel threatened.

God, she was gorgeous.

Her hair was a red beacon in the smoky gloom, and her fair skin had been kissed by the summer sun. Her lips were full, pouting, and those breasts stretched thin the fabric of her shirt; her nipples protesting the chill of air-conditioning. He had never been a believer in love at first sight, but lust...this was definitely lust at first sight.

When she looked up, Scott turned away. He didn't want her to catch him staring.

A raised firepit filled the center of the bar, its walls constructed of gray stone and a black metal grill laid across the top. Scott longed to smell fresh New England lobsters and fish being seared over flame, but tonight the fires were dormant, leaving his nose to the cigarette stench that clouded the air.

A Wurlitzer juke box glowed yellow in the corner, bubbling, singing Billy Joel's "Downeaster 'Alexa'" as two men in Hawaiian shirts and jeans played pool. There were small groups scattered among the tables and booths; people talking, drinking, laughing. Everyone seemed to know everyone else, everyone but Scott and the beauty that sat two stools over.

The bartender wiped a wine glass clean with the towel that hung from his waist and turned to Scott. He was a tall man, muscular, his head covered by a thin lawn of crew-cut, his arms marked with tattoos. The white muscle shirt he wore had the bar's logo printed on its chest. The Sand Bar. "What can I getcha?"

"Miller High Life." Scott glanced at the woman on the far stool. Her mug was empty. "Miss?"

She didn't look up.

"Miss?" he repeated.

Her eyes rose, found his. "Yes?"

"What are you drinking?"

"Killian's," she said absently. Her voice was soft, breathy.

Scott smiled. *An Irish red for the red-head.* "Like another?"

She nodded.

He turned back to the bartender. "And a Killian's for the lady."

The man looked Scott up and down, then glanced at the woman, his expression one of disapproval.

"Is there a problem?" Scott wanted to know.

The bartender walked away without a word.

"Thanks," the woman said, still fascinated by a foamy residue in the well of her glass.

"Don't mention it. I'm Scott, by the way." He held out his hand to her.

She looked at it for a moment before shaking it. "Sue. Sue O'Connor."

Now Scott moved to the stool next to her, thinking that with a name like O'Connor, she *had* to be Irish. "So, Sue O'Connor, what's a beautiful girl like you doing here all alone?"

She laughed bitterly. "That the best you could come up with?"

He chuckled; ran a hand across his mouth and chin, feeling the prickle of goatee. "Pretty lame, huh? Well, for what it's worth, you *are* beautiful." He hoped the remark would coax a smile to her ruby lips, but it garnered nothing. "If you don't want company, just say the word and I'll leave you alone."

"There's nobody from this God-forsaken island I'd want to sit with," Sue told him.

Scott gave an understanding nod, cursing himself for believing he had a chance. When he stood, however, she reached out and grabbed him by the arm.

"You're not an islander," she said.

"That obvious, huh?" He settled back onto the stool. "Yeah, I'm just here for the day, fishing with friends."

"Catch anything?"

Scott shook his head. "We were out there most of the afternoon, but we couldn't find any fish willing to throw themselves on our hooks."

"So..." She looked to either side of him and smiled, sending tingles down his spine. "Where're your friends now?"

"They got frustrated, went on home."

When the bartender brought their drinks, Scott could not help but study the man's arm. Drawn monsters, with sharp teeth and equally sharp claws, rose from blue flames, crawling up his forearm toward a golden pitchfork that had been etched onto his bicep. The artwork was amazingly detailed, like Dante's wet dream. Scott could make out individual scales on the creatures' colorful skins, could see the gleam in their black eyes, the sparkle of light on their glistening fangs.

They took their beers from the painted man and he eyed them across his shoulder as he moved away.

"What's *his* problem?" Scott asked aloud, though not loud enough for the bartender to hear.

"Craig?" She rolled her eyes. "Where do I start? Used to work here for his Dad when I got outta high school. Waitressing, mostly. Did it 'til I got a shop of my own."

"He...uh, looks like a pretty rough character, demons and pitchforks on his arm and everything."

"That's not a pitchfork," Sue corrected with a grin. "It's a trident, Colonial Bay High School's logo. Craig was a lineman on the football team. Pretty hard-core."

Scott took another look the man's arm, trying not to be obvious about it. He saw the symbol clearly now. A trident. Neptune's spear. And he realized something else: the blue tongues of flame weren't really flames at all. They were meant to be a splash of ocean waves. "I've seen guys get tats of their college team before, but never high school."

She frowned. "High school's 'bout as far as people get around here."

"Sorry."

"Me too." Sue looked into her beer again, her finger tracing the rim of the mug.

Scott drank from his long-necked bottle and decided to quickly change the subject. "What do you sell?"

She blinked. "What?"

"In your store?—fudge?—artwork?"

"Well..." Her face tried to match the color of her hair. "I run the Shirt Shack."

"The Shirt Shack?"

"Ayuh. I put iron-on decals on shirts for the tourists. You've probably seen 'em around. 'Colonial Bay: America's Home by the Sea.'"

Scott snickered into his bottle.

"What's so funny?"

"Sorry," he told her. He didn't want to blow this. "It's just that I haven't seen one of those iron-on decal places since I was a kid."

"You sayin' we're behind the times?"

"I...*No*, I—"

"We are, you know." Sue leaned over to him. The scent of her perfume was incredible. A trace of smile returned to her lips, but her voice remained quite serious. "Sometimes, this island feels like a damn prison."

Scott took another drink of his beer, grateful that she wasn't pissed at him, then said, "I know exactly what you mean. I answer phones for an insurance company. Feels like I'm just shackled to that desk, listening to people bitch all day long about this and that. Not really what I wanted to do after graduation."

"Beats the hell outta standing over a steaming hot press ten hours straight." She emptied her mug. "Wasn't too bad today, though."

"Not a lot of call for iron-on shirts?"

"Not a lot of *tourists*. Boy's body washed up on the beach this morning. Shark attack. Scared 'em all off."

"Our captain mentioned something about that." Scott nodded at the set of serrated teeth that filled the wall behind them. "Had us all hoping we'd catch *Jaws* or something."

She giggled, pointing to the toothy yawn. "I can just see you out there, trying to reel *that* onto Ed Keel's little tug."

Scott closed one eye and attempted a pirate voice, "Aye, we'd need a bigger boat."

At that, they both burst into full-blown laughter.

Craig glanced up, stone-faced, then returned his attention to the drink he was mixing, the golden trident growing larger as he flexed his arm.

Scott continued to nurse his drink. "You know, the Hawaiians used to worship sharks."

Her smile widened. "No, I didn't. Is that where you're from?"

"Hawaii?" He chuckled at that. "No, no. I was born and raised in Indiana. It's true though, saw it on the Discovery Channel. Each island had their own shark god."

"Did *you* know sharks never get cancer?"

He'd heard that before, but he didn't want to appear too smart for her. He did his best Johnny Carson: "I did not know that."

"Nobody's sure how long they live. They could be fucking immortal for all we know."

"Now there's a scary thought."

Her smile evaporated. "People think human beings are masters of the whole damn universe. I sit in my store, day in and day out, and I watch them file off ferryboats like stupid cattle. They bring their cell phones, their Gameboys or...what are they now?...PS2s, their i-pods and boom boxes, beach blankets and sunblock...trying to turn the shore into some backyard barbecue. Drop them in the middle of the ocean without all their crap, they'll find out how nature really works: predators and prey. Something will eat them up and shit them out and that'll be that."

Scott looked once more to the wall of teeth, trying for a moment to imagine a world where such monsters were possible. He shook his head, smiling. "Better not let you write Colonial Bay's next slogan. Instead of spending a day on your beach, you'll have people in bed pissing themselves."

Sue laughed, her grin once more in bloom. She put her elbow on the bar and held her cheek in her hand, looking at him with deep blue eyes. "Wanna buy me another drink, Scott?"

Another drink became two more drinks.

Finally, Sue looked up at him, licked the residue of alcohol from her exquisite lips, and said the magic words: "Let's get outta here."

Scott was quick to produce several twenties from his wallet. He slapped them on the counter and gave Craig a salute. The bartender looked as if he were about to say something, but he remained silent, his eyes following them as they exited the bar and walked into the night.

"So...are we going to your place?" Scott hoped he didn't sound too anxious.

"I got a better idea." She led him to an alleyway, pulling at his hand, urging him to enter.

"What?" he asked. "In *there*?"

"Why not?"

Reasons "why not" leapt to the forefront of his brain. It was dark, sure to be dirty, smelly. And then, for the first time in years, his college roommate barged into his mind with one of those wild sex tales, telling Scott how he'd met a girl in some night club, then immediately had sex with her in a Men's room stall. Scott thought his friend had been full of shit, that the adventures he described were Penthouse Forum fantasies, nothing more. Things like that didn't happen in reality, or more accurately, they didn't happen to *him*. Until now. Scott glanced around, then looked back at Sue, at her full lips and large breasts, and he followed her willingly into the shadows.

She leaned against the wall, tugging at his shirt. "Come here, lover."

He looked up at the Sand Bar logo painted across the brick, and stopped her. "Did you date Craig?"

Her eyes lowered, then rose to meet his. "Does it matter?"

Scott took a step back. Her ex-boyfriend. It all made sense now...the man's dirty looks, her eagerness. This was about hurting Craig. Perhaps he'd cheated on her when they were together, and now she wanted to screw someone right under his nose. He shot a nervous glance toward the bar's service entrance, then looked back at Sue. "Look, I don't want the guy to come out here and cut my balls off."

Her smile widened, her teeth reflecting dim light from a bulb above the door. "You don't have to worry about that." She grabbed the neck of Scott's T-shirt, pulled him to her. When he was close enough, she kissed his ear, whispering, "He's a coward."

Scott's nose rested against the nape of her neck, and the sweet smell of her perfume was now overpowering, stirring him to arousal. He touched her breast, feeling its softness beneath his palm. She sighed, and then their lips met in a passionate embrace, their tongues frolicking like old friends. When he reached down to unbutton the fly of her jeans, she made no protest. Scott's fingers traced the waistband of her panties, then slid beneath their silky fabric.

Her skin was smooth.

*She shaves*, he thought, intrigued, and then he felt something else, something long and snake-like. Scott's eyes jerked open, his stomach wanting to heave.

*Holy shit...she's a* he.

He broke free of her kiss, his revulsion instantly replaced by an even greater dread. The thing in her pants, whatever it was, coiled around his wrist, holding it in a death grip. He had the horrid sensation of something else, moist and slimy, slithering its way up his arm, and when he looked at his hand, Sue's jeans and underwear slid down her thighs, revealing the writhing nest of tentacles at her crotch. They constricted their muscles, preventing him from pulling away.

Scott's disbelieving stare returned to Sue's face, finding it no longer human. Color had abandoned her eyes to darkness. Her bright red hair was gone, her naked scalp expanding, ballooning into a huge, pulsating sack. Her nose and mouth had also disappeared, covered over by a living beard of whips and tentacles.

*A squid*, his mind muttered. *She's got a squid for a head.* He closed his eyes, wanting this to be no more than a drunken hallucination.

"Everyone on this island's a coward," the squid-woman said, her voice a wet gurgle. "Everyone but me."

Her whips lashed out, embracing Scott's skull, their thorny suction cups ripping at his flesh. When he saw the sharpened beak of her mouth, Scott Jarvis screamed.

Their shadows formed one horrid shape on the brick wall, and his screaming came to an abrupt end.

---

The Service door opened and Craig stepped into the alley, a bulging Hefty bag in each hand. He tossed them into the dumpster, then turned to find Sue O'Connor bridging the boundary between light and shadow, her face buried in the neck of her fresh kill.

"I didn't think you'd actually do it," the bartender said, a cocktail of fear and anger mixing in his voice.

Sue swallowed a chunk of the dead man's flesh before speaking. "It's what the gods created me to do. I think you've all forgotten that."

Craig said nothing, but his hand went to his arm, his fingers stroking the trident symbol, the sign of the old ones, the mark of the creators.

"Don't worry," she assured him, her facial tentacles dancing in the air. "I was careful. He wasn't married. He lived alone. Nobody will miss him."

"He woulda told you anything to get in your pants." Craig took a step forward, his eyes fixed on the body's torn throat...on the blood. He stopped suddenly and lowered his head, still rubbing his tattoo as if it were causing him pain. "What if someone comes looking for him?"

"People go missing at sea all the time," Sue reminded.

The bartender opened his mouth as if to argue, then closed it again. What could he say? Nothing. She was right and he knew it. Sue had used no knife, no bullet. Her body had been her only weapon. If her leftovers washed ashore, there was nowhere to point a suspicious finger except back to the ocean, and the sea kept its secrets well.

Sue held the body out to him. "You know...there's enough here to share."

Craig's head snapped up, his eyes surveying the darkness of the alley. They were alone; alone with the warm meat, the glorious stench of freshly spilled blood. His nostrils flared, drinking it in, and then his face leapt forward, forming the pointed snout of a shark. He opened his mouth, displaying jagged, serrated teeth, and bent down, taking the dead man's leg in his jaws, tearing calf muscle from bone in one greedy bite.

Sue O'Connor smiled as she watched Craig feed, thinking of the ferryboats that would bring fresh tourists from the mainland in the morning, hoping this was not the last time the bartender would join her for a meal.

# EINSTEIN'S SLINGSHOT

Deputy Jackson was scared. He had a rifle to protect him, but Bill could tell he was scared just the same. The man was sweating so much that his beige Shannon County Sheriff's uniform looked as if he'd bathed in it, and his eyes darted back and forth, like he was watching a tennis match play out. Worst of all, he was bouncing on the balls of his feet, ready to leap out of hiding at any moment.

Bill focused on the key ring that hung from Jackson's belt, hoping the deputy wouldn't get himself killed.

The dark-haired mother sat against the wall behind them, her light-haired daughter cradled in her lap. Light-haired daughter looked six, maybe seven years old, and she sobbed wildly. Dark-haired mother held the girl tightly to her breast, trying to muffle cries of anguish she longed to accompany.

"Can't you shut her up?" the bleeding guy in the corner asked. He was dressed in the tattered remains of a gray business suit, a Taggart Labs identification badge clipped to his breast pocket. The I.D. said the man's name was Ken Hobbs, but the clean, smiling face in the picture looked like a distant relative of the man who wore it.

Dark-haired mother replied with an angry glance that shot through her tears.

"They'll hear her," Hobbs warned. "They'll get us."

"Be quiet."

Bill looked over his shoulder at the young couple. It was the boyfriend who'd spoken. He was a buff kid, just shy of legal drinking age, and his hand was fisted. His girlfriend was a cute redhead with not much meat on her bones. After what they'd all just seen, Bill thought that was probably to her advantage.

Hobbs opened his mouth to reply, then thought better of it. He wiped at the gash in his forehead, then hugged his knees, pulling himself up into a ball, trying to become as small as possible.

Bill's eyes went back to Jackson, happy to see the deputy was still being cool, then peered between two half-eaten cakes in the display case they were using for cover.

At the entrance to the bookstore, a red Liberty SUV was parked on the wreckage of the foyer, its grill and bumper badly dented, its hood covered in a frost of plaster and broken glass. Several bookcases had been turned over, their contents fanning out across the floor. One of the books lay open, as if the reader left his or her studies in a hurry. The printing was illegible, partly because it was too far away, and partly because the pages were stamped by a bloody, three-toed footprint.

What was left of the Liberty's driver lay strewn between the café counter and the downed bookcases. He'd been husband to the dark-haired mother against the wall, father to her sobbing little light-haired girl. When he saw the attack coming, the man pushed his daughter into his wife's arms and purchased their escape with his life. More than an hour had passed since then, but Bill could still hear that man's dying screams. Thankfully, the power was out and their view of the remains was kept faint.

Bill reached his hand up onto the counter and his other hand was dragged along for the ride. The handcuff's chain rubbed the metal edge of the display case, making a slight rasp that drew Jackson's attention.

The deputy lowered his rifle, its barrel staring right at Bill's nose. The muscles in Jackson's neck were tight ropes beneath his skin as he spoke, "What the hell are you doin'?"

Slowly, Bill brought his hand back, his fingers wrapped around a scone. He tossed it to the dark-haired mother and said, "Maybe some food will quiet her down."

She nodded, offering the sweet to her daughter. "Here, Hannah," she whispered.

The light-haired girl, Hannah, began nibbling as if programmed to do so. As Bill watched her eat, he found himself wondering if she'd been given any food since the quake.

There was an odd whistling sound, like a teakettle ready to spew steam, and Jackson returned his aim to the darkened sales floor.

The animal came into view again. It was as tall as the bookcases that surrounded it. Walking by, you might think it was some kind of display, something a marketing exec had sent the store to plug an upcoming fantasy, but it was all too real. It was adorned with brightly colored feathers, yet it was like no bird Bill had ever seen. Decorative quills trimmed its long arms, and the three slender, scaly fingers on each of its hands danced in the air as if it were typing. Serrated teeth stabbed from the gums of a crocodile snout, and above this mouth, its eyes burned in the darkness like the glowing embers of a bonfire. They were cat's eyes, red circles split down the middle by black wounds.

Bill's own eyes drifted to the thing's feet. The second toe of each foot sprouted a six-inch-long talon, a scythe to cut down its prey. Little Hannah's father was screaming again in his mind, and Bill forced himself to look away.

Hobbs stared at the sobbing girl, his face a taut expression of horror, his eyes wide and manic. "It'll hear her," he warned again. "It'll—"

Jackson rose up and fired his rifle.

The sound of the blast ricocheted off the bistro tile. Hannah clapped her hands over her ears and her mother screamed. Hobbs jerked back, pressing himself flat against the wall. Bill could hear the boyfriend shouting obscenities behind him, but he didn't turn to see what the young couple was doing. His eyes were firmly planted on Jackson, on the keys that swung wildly from the deputy's belt.

Jackson's shell missed its target entirely. It struck the corner of a bookcase, creating a blizzard of splinters and confetti, drawing the creature's attention toward the café. Long feathers on the back of its neck stood erect, forming a threatening peacock mane. The teakettle whistle became a much deeper roar, and the animal charged, arms outstretched, teeth bared. When its feet smacked the tile, the floor shook.

Jackson leapt the counter, his legs sweeping coffee cups and powdered creamer onto the floor, and fired off another shot. His bullet cut through the air just behind the rushing predator, shattering a hanging globe light.

Bill wondered how many shells the rifle could hold, and then he saw the animal hop up on one foot, slashing Jackson's abdomen open with a single swipe of its sickle claw.

The deputy's innards unraveled. They struck the floor with a wet slap and he followed them down, landing on his knees in front of the steaming heap. With his final breath, Jackson thrust the rifle barrel against the creature's scaly chin and tugged on the trigger. This time, his shell hit home and the top of the animal's head erupted onto the ceiling. Jackson and the creature fell in opposite directions, both victorious killers, both defeated prey.

Bill turned away, but the young guy behind him stared at the carnage with a look of amazement, his redheaded girl-friend crying on his shoulder. The dark-haired mother's eyes were closed. She continued to sway back and forth, rocking Hannah in her arms as she sobbed. In the corner, even Hobbs had tears.

"I'm sorry," he said, then fell silent.

Time passed slowly. How much time, Bill really couldn't say. They'd taken his watch when he went into lock-up, and the clock on the wall was stuck on 11:15, same time as the quake. All he knew for certain was that the room was growing darker as the sunlight slowly died.

He turned toward Deputy Jackson. The key ring hung across the man's lifeless rump, daring him to come out and get it.

"Hey," the boyfriend said, tapping Bill roughly on the shoulder of his orange jumpsuit.

"What?"

"What'd you do?"

"Does that really matter right now?"

"It might," he said, trying to sound tough in front of the redhead. "I see you looking at those keys over there. Before you find a way to get free of those cuffs, I think I'd like to know why you're wearing them."

Bill ran his hand over his goatee. "Son, don't you think you got better things to be scared of than me?"

The boy looked at the dead creature through the glass display case, at the rows of teeth in its yawning snout. "I suppose so."

"We're gonna have to work together if we wanna get through this alive." Bill held up his shackled hands. "And I'd be a helluva lot more useful to you if you'd help me get these things off."

The redhead tugged on the boy's arm. Drops of blood spoiled the white fabric of her Hard Rock Café T-shirt, but she didn't appear to be wounded. "Don't you dare, Ryan! He could be a rapist or a child molester or something."

She looked back at little Hannah and her dark-haired mother for emphasis.

"Ma'am, right now I'm just a guy who doesn't want his ass chewed off."

She glared at him. "Well that's exactly what'll happen if you walk out there. You want to go after those keys, go right ahead. Don't expect us to commit suicide with you."

The others stared at him in silence, their eyes all expressing the same sentiment the redhead had given voice. They knew they couldn't stay cowering in this little bookstore café forever, but none wanted to be the first to venture out. Bill was going to be their hat on the stick, and they would wait to see what happened to him before they made a move.

"Fine." His leg muscles groaned in protest as he stood and stepped out onto the tile. There was a light breeze blowing in around the Liberty at the front of the store, but the air was still quite humid. He blinked, then wiped a stinging drop of sweat from his eyes, the chain of his shackles jingling far too loudly to suit him.

As a thief, Bill was used to moving stealthily. He would

stake out a house, watch it, go through trash the owners chucked to the curb each Tuesday, all to prepare himself for what he might find when he forced open a window or picked the lock on a door. When he decided to cross that line, he wanted no surprises. Were there dogs?—cameras?—a loaded gun in a bedside drawer? You needed to know things like that before you put your hand in the cookie jar, not after. After could get you killed, or at least a "go directly to jail" card.

Whistling sounded in the distance.

The tingling hand of fear gripped Bill by the balls and his stomach sank. He stood frozen, listening. After what seemed like an eternity, he heard it again. It was more distant now, and he realized it was coming from somewhere outside the store. He found himself wondering how many of those creatures were beyond the smashed doorway, standing between here and the highway with their teeth and their scythes, but he quickly shook it off. If he thought about it too much, he'd find himself crying in a corner like Hobbs, or worse: he'd run off screaming and end up like poor Deputy Jackson over there.

After a moment of nothing but the beat of his own pulse in his ear, Bill resumed his slide along the café wall. He focused on the rifle, on the keys. They seemed a long way away from him, but he was there in four running steps.

Bill grabbed the rifle, checked the chamber to make sure it still held a shell, then knelt down and yanked the ring free of Deputy Jackson's belt. He stabbed keys into his cuffs, their too large teeth scratching the metal around the hole. Finally, one of them slid inside the lock, turning with a clicking sound that was fine music. His hand jerked free of the manacle and he stood up, aiming the rifle in all directions, finding nothing. The creature trapped in the store with them had been alone.

"The coast is clear," Bill proclaimed.

The boy, Ryan, moved out from behind the counter and

walked over to the animal's body, the redhead latched to his back like a lamprey. He kicked its foot with his boot, watching its bloody talon rock to and fro. "We saw one of these things climb a telephone pole this morning," he said. "It was using these big claws like a repairman's cleats. Went right up the pole, fast as could be, and jumped into a second floor window." He chuckled a bit at that, but Bill could see he was unnerved. "As we were running, I could...they were screaming, the people inside. We could hear them screaming."

Bill frowned, trying to picture one of these creatures climbing in through somebody's window, then worked the second lock. "The quake hit, and my bunk threw me like a mechanical bull. Then the overhead fluorescents blow, and it's raining sparks on us." His shackles dropped to the floor and he rubbed his worn, aching wrists, smearing the blood that encircled them. "Next thing I know, these monsters are rushin' the cells, pushin' their feathery mugs between the bars. They were jumpin' up on people's backs as we ran down the hall to get away."

He knelt down beside Jackson's corpse. *I may not have liked you, but wherever you are, thanks for gettin' me outta that hell.* Bill dropped the keys and searched the deputy's pockets, finding more shells. He took them.

The redhead had her hand across her chin, her fingers and thumb pressing dents into her own cheeks. "What are these things?"

"Looks like a deinonychus," Ryan said. "Either that or a Utah raptor." He realized they were looking at him as if he were speaking in tongues. "I'm studying paleontology. We go out on digs all the time. There's some great fossil beds around here." He nervously rubbed the back of his neck. "Anyway, this looks like one of the dinosaurs we've studied. Lived here about 144 million years ago."

"Dinosaur?" The redhead swallowed. "But...it's got feathers."

"Dinosaurs had feathers, Kim," Ryan assured her. "My professor likes to teach all the new theories, the stuff that gets old school scientists all pissed off. T-Rex was a scavenger. Dinosaurs were birds. This looks like one of the new-wave paintings he's showed us. But, I mean...it's not really a *dinosaur*. It can't be."

Laughter came from behind the counter.

It was Hobbs. There were deep, dark wrinkles under his eyes, like fault lines in his porcelain face.

"We did it," he said abruptly. "We brought them here."

Bill thought the day's events were driving this man to insanity, if they hadn't already left him stranded there. Then he remembered the Taggart Labs ID badge. "You a scientist?"

Hobbs shook his head. "Public Relations. I write press releases, wine and dine senators...get investors laid." He gave another half-hearted giggle. "It was supposed to be a simple test. We were just going to give them a taste of what it could do."

The redhead, Kim, tightened her hold on Ryan's arm. "What *what* could do?"

"The SK64...Einstein's Slingshot." Hobbs smiled, sending a sudden chill through Bill like a gust of arctic wind. "It was a brand new propulsion system we...*they* designed for NASA, was going to revolutionize the whole space program. 'Mars in minutes' they kept chanting."

"How?" Ryan wanted to know.

Hobbs looked annoyed. "How the hell should I know? Wormholes, tachyons...the guys in lab coats were throwing words around like they meant something. I don't know what they were doing. I just know they fucked up big time."

He wiped at his eyes again with the back of his hand.

Beside him, the dark-haired mother was still rocking to and fro. Hannah had thankfully found sleep, but she was squirming even in her unconsciousness.

"We had the money people there," Hobbs went on to say, "the chairman of the Senate committee, everybody who was anybody. They had a chair hooked to the engine and a chimp belted to the chair. It was just supposed to be a short trip...once around the globe, just like a boomerang..."

His voice trailed off and his sunken eyes grew vacant.

Bill moved to the counter, his hand gripping the butt of the rifle so tightly it grew numb. "What happened?"

Hobbs snapped back into his recollection. "Somebody screamed about a systems overload, that the field was unstable. Next thing I know, computers are exploding and there's this huge...wall of energy, like a big bubble of blue electricity that kept expanding. The earth started shaking, and we all ran. We ran from the bubble, then we ran from..." He tilted his head toward the dinosaur's corpse. "We ran from those things over there. The fuckheads opened a door in space and time, and let these... these *monsters* waltz right through it."

Bill closed his eyes, thinking of all the crappy sci-fi movies he'd seen as a kid. Evidently, the white coats at Taggart Labs had never watched them.

Ryan made a bold announcement: "We have to go turn it off."

"We don't gotta do shit except get outta Dodge." Bill indicated the Liberty blocking the entrance. "I say we just drive. When we get someplace safe, you can tell whoever you want."

"Listen to him," Kim said, pulling on Ryan's beefy arm. Bill found it amusing that the girl now cared about what this "rapist" had to say. "You don't always have to be the hero, y'know. Let the state police or the National Guard take care of it."

"I'm not going back out there," Hobbs told them. "We should just stay put and wait for help."

Bill rested the rifle barrel on his shoulder. "It took 'em a week to get help to New Orleans after Katrina. Wanna hang out here with those things for a week?"

Hobbs said nothing. He rested his head on his knees.

Kim spoke up again, "I tried using my cell phone to call for help, but I can't get any bars. I dial a number and the screen just says 'no service.'"

"The quake probably took out some signal towers." Ryan rubbed her back and nodded at Hobbs. "Or that weird energy he's talking about might be causing some kind of interference."

Bill reached out to the dark-haired mother on the floor, gently touching her arm. "What's your name?"

She blinked, then said, "Sarah."

"How much gas in your Jeep, Sarah?"

She shook her head. "Mark filled it last."

"Is it even drivable?" Kim asked.

Bill glanced at the damaged grill, then shrugged. "Won't know for sure 'til I go over and start 'er up."

He tilted his head to glance at the watch on Kim's wrist. It said eight o'clock. They had about an hour of daylight left. "We'll give it a shot first thing in the morning."

"You mean..." Kim's eyes widened. "...spend the night here?"

"The quake could've knocked out a bridge, dropped live electrical wires everywhere, or it might've brought down a whole fuckin' building and blocked the street. During the day, we can see those things before we're right on top of them." He looked at Ryan. "How well can dinosaurs see in the dark?"

The boy shrugged. "You can't tell things like that from

fossils, but it looks like our friend here has alligator eyes. Alligators have great night vision."

Bill nodded and turned back to Kim. "That's what I thought."

She ran her fingers through her red hair. "Well...how are we going to even see in here without power?"

"I'd say make a pile of books and light a fire," Bill said, "but that might attract them."

"What about these?" Ryan reached out to a spinner rack next to the café counter. It was filled with bookmarks, batteries, and small reading lamps. He took one of the lights off its hook and tossed it to Bill.

Bill looked the package over and nodded. "Cool."

"What happens if they get in here again?" Kim asked, nodding at the rifle in Bill's hands. "We only have the one gun."

*And not more than a handful of shells,* Bill was about to add, but stopped himself. He pointed behind the counter. "This place serves food, right? There's gotta be some knives back there."

Kim offered him a skeptical glance, as if to say she didn't intend to get that close to the creatures, but she walked over to the drawers and rummaged around. She found a butcher's knife and two long, serrated blades used for slicing bread and bagels.

"I'll take first watch," Bill told them. His eyes skidded over Sarah and Hannah, landing squarely on Hobbs.

"Don't look at me!" the man whined.

"Kim and I can stand guard the rest of the night," Ryan quickly volunteered. "We're used to pulling all-nighters for school anyway."

Bill was still glaring at Hobbs. "Sounds like a plan."

Within an hour, the sun had completely deserted them, leaving the store like a cave. Bill sat at one of the bistro tables, his eyes on the front windows, on the empty street beyond. He ate a slice of spinach quiche from the display case with one hand and held the rifle firmly in the other. They said real men didn't eat quiche, but *they* had never gone a day without food.

What struck him most was the silence. No traffic noise. No police sirens—a sound his ears had become quite tuned to over the years. And, of course with no power, there was no whir of air-conditioning or ceiling fans. Occasionally, he would hear the distant teakettle whistle of the animals on the hunt and his finger would instinctively move to the trigger, but they never drew near.

Moonlight cut through the gloom, making the faces of buildings across the street plainly visible. His attention shifted from one darkened window to the next. How many people were hiding up in those rooms?—under beds?—in closets? He had a nightmare vision of dinosaurs scrambling up telephone poles to eat them and quickly shook it off.

About the time Bill felt himself starting to doze, Ryan and Kim arrived to take their turn at watch. He reluctantly handed them the rifle and used his reading light to find a place to sleep.

---

"Mister?"

A female voice, soft and somehow familiar, filtered through the veil of slumber.

It was followed by a male voice, also familiar, "I think he said his name was Bill."

"Wake up, Bill."

He became aware of a hand on his shoulder, shaking him, and when he opened his eyes, the backlit shape of a woman with a knife startled him to consciousness.

She held up her free hand. "It's me, Kim. There's something in here with us."

Her words were like a splash of cold water on his brain. Bill remembered where he was, remembered the situation he was in, and was instantly on his feet. He followed Kim onto the tiled floor of the café where Ryan stood with the book light and rifle.

Bill looked at the silhouetted Liberty at the front of the store. "Where?"

"Listen," Ryan told him.

And then he heard it: a rustling sound, like someone quickly flipping through the books that littered the sales floor. "You hear their whistle yet?"

Ryan shook his head. "We heard it outside, but not in here. This is something different."

*Something different.* Bill's stomach knotted and came loose in spasms. "Give me the gun."

Ryan turned it over, and Bill took a step toward the bookcases. The soft, clandestine patter of tiny feet stopped him in his tracks. Whatever was out there, it had moved from the paper strewn across the floor to the wooden cases themselves.

"Sounds like rats."

"Rats?" Kim's shaking hands held out the butcher's knife like a sword.

Bill could not help but grin. The idea of overgrown mice was somehow more frightening to this girl than dinosaurs run amok. "Welcome to life in the big city, darlin'."

Lightning fast movement in the corner of his eye, something long and snake-like.

Whatever this thing was, Bill knew now that it was no rat. He took two steps back, aiming his lamp at the floor and surrounding walls, hearing the stealthy rustle become a rattling, banging sound. It was coming from above. Bill lifted his light and glimpsed a dark shape moving quickly across the ceiling tiles. At first, he thought it *was* a snake, then he saw the legs...hundreds of tiny legs.

Bill aimed his rifle and fired. Exploded fiberglass rained, bringing the overgrown millipede down with it. The insect writhed on the flooring, then scurried toward Kim. She screamed, crashed back through the bistro tables and chairs, and then it was on top of her, long stalks of antennae batting against her chest, huge pincers opening wide.

Ryan was at her side in a flash. He grabbed hold of the segmented exoskeleton and yanked it off his girlfriend's torso, countless tiny limbs swimming in the air as he peeled it back.

Kim's screams turned to primitive grunts. She swung at the insect with her butcher's knife, hacking into its thin body as if it were the green limb of a tree, then stabbed its tender under-belly again and again, dark fluid dowsing her, further staining her Hard Rock shirt.

Bill ran over to help. The millipede's legs were barbed and they had latched onto Kim's jeans. He dropped the rifle, took hold of the thing's ass, and helped Ryan pull. When she was free of it, Kim scrambled to her feet, tears clearing paths in the grime that now soiled her face.

They pinned the insect against the tile, and it continued to struggle in their grip. Its antennae waved around wildly, its pincers opening and closing with an odd clucking sound.

"Shoot it!" Ryan begged.

Before Bill could reach for the rifle, Kim grabbed hold of one of the bistro chairs. She brought it crashing down on the bug's head, then picked it back up and repeated the clubbing until the millipede stopped writhing.

"It's okay, honey," Ryan told her. He rose up and held her tightly to him. "It's dead now. It's okay."

"It's not okay," she cried. "I wanna go home. Take me home."

Ryan smoothed her red hair with his hand. "I know, Babe."

"We're out of here at dawn," Bill promised her.

She lifted her head from Ryan's shoulder and glared at him. "If we live that long."

Bill heard whimpering and shined his book light across the café, thinking he would find Hannah crying in her mother's lap. Instead, he saw Hobbs rocking back and forth in his corner. The man's hands were planted firmly over his ears.

Rage bubbled up inside of Bill, and he resisted the urge to run over, hoist Hobbs up by his tie, and beat the living shit out of him. Hobbs may not have opened Pandora's box himself, but his hands were far from clean. Whatever "Einstein's Sling-shot" was, Hobbs had better pray it didn't fling anything else at them before sunrise.

What little remained of the night was uneventful, but none of them were able to get much rest.

At first light, Bill slid behind the Liberty's wheel and found the key still in the ignition. He turned it, hearing the engine purr, then checked the gauges. The gas needle hung half-way between empty and a quarter of a tank. He prayed it would be enough.

The others made their way to the vehicle as fast as they could. Ryan pushed Hobbs through the passenger door, then helped the women climb up into the backseat. When they were all within the protection of the SUV, Bill grabbed the gearshift and threw it into reverse.

Glass slid from the hood like slabs of ice, plaster dust

billowed around the tires, and the cab bounced as the Jeep retreated over the curb. When all four wheels were firmly on the street, Bill floored the accelerator, driving east. The squeal of rubber on asphalt sounded like one of the animals attacking, prompting Hannah to scream.

Unseen fires sent black smoke drifting across the road. Bill sped through the cloud to find deserted cars parked wildly along curbs and stalled down the center of the street, some with their doors left open. He turned the wheel to the right, then to the left, swerving around and between these abandoned vehicles. A station wagon sat atop the ruined stump of a water hydrant, but there was no geyser. The car's owner stared out at Bill from a mangled face glazed in blood. He couldn't tell if it had been a man or a woman.

A loud beep thankfully pulled Bill's attention away from the carnage, and he saw a tiny red gas pump ignite on the dash.

"Shit."

The Marathon station on the corner of Washington and Montgomery appeared deserted. Bill pulled the Liberty up to the Full Service pumps, eyeing the convenience store and garages for any sign of movement. There were three service bays. The center one was a gaping mouth, but he could see nothing but darkness within.

He turned off the engine, grabbing his rifle and door handle before looking into the backseat. "Ryan, on three, I want you to get behind the wheel."

The boy nodded.

"One...two..." Bill took one last glance around the lot, saw nothing, and went on. "Three."

He threw his door open and ran around the Liberty, staring across the barrel of his rifle at the cavernous garage.

When Ryan climbed into the driver's seat, Bill backed up to the passenger's side window.

"I got to go into the station for a bit," he said. "Ryan, anything comes up, I want you to drive off like a bat outta Hell. Got me?"

The boy held onto the steering wheel with pale knuckles. "I can't just leave you here."

Hobbs spoke up, "Then let *me* drive!"

The man from Taggart Labs stank of fear. It wafted through the open window in waves. Ryan was athletic, but if Hobbs panicked...Bill could see him overpowering the boy, driving away with the girls along for the ride. He couldn't let that happen.

Bill opened the passenger door. "Get out."

"What?" Hobbs sat up straight in his seat.

"You heard me."

"Not me." He grabbed the Liberty's drink holder as if it were a life preserver. "I'm staying right here."

"I said out!" Bill spun the rifle around toward Hobbs' sweaty face.

The man turned ashen. He held up his hands as if he were being robbed, slid from his seat, and stepped away.

Bill slammed the door, then motioned with his rifle. "After you."

Hobbs walked slowly toward the open garage. "Why don't you just pump the damn gas?"

"Because there's no power. No power means no pumps."

"Then why are we even here?"

"You're gonna help me siphon gas from the underground tanks."

"I don't know how to..." The protest died in Hobbs' throat.

Bill lowered his eyes to see what the man was looking at. A

wide trail of blood ran from the garage floor onto the asphalt. It looked as if someone had been dragged off.

"Jesus..." Hobbs' tone made it sound as if the name had truly been offered in prayer.

"Come on." Bill gave him a little push between the shoulder blades to get him moving again.

They stepped cautiously into the darkened garage, finding a white Ford Taurus up on a lift. What was left of the car's mechanic lay on the floor below, his glazed eyes staring up at the undercarriage with sleepy fascination. Everything below the man's gnawed ribcage was gone, carried away, leaving the bloody path they'd found at the door. According to the patch on his torn coveralls, his name had been Jake.

"Where..." Hobbs put a hand across his mouth and swallowed, his forehead crinkling as he spoke. "Where'd they take his legs?"

"Don't worry about it," Bill told him. "Let's just get what we need and go before they come back for the rest."

They continued deeper into the garage.

Bill started opening drawers until he found a length of rubber tubing. There was a long, black prybar hanging on the back wall. He grabbed it and turned back to Hobbs.

The man was still looking at poor Jake's remains, his pale face almost glowing in the dimness.

"Don't just stand there." Bill threw him the prybar. "See if you can find a big gas can."

Hobbs looked around as if he were lost, then walked to some shelving units.

Bill moved to the opposite end of the garage bay, finding a row of lockers. Most were bolted with combination locks, but there was one he could access. Inside, he found a blue mechanic's coverall with Jake's name on the breast. He smiled. After a quick survey of his surroundings, Bill put down his rifle, leaning it against the lockers for support. He then stripped off his prisoner's garb and slid his legs and arms into the new clothing.

"Found a gas can in the—" Hobbs looked suddenly shocked. "What the hell are you doing?"

"Changing. We run into cops, I can't very well show up wearing prison orange and expect them to just let me go my merry way."

"How can you think about that now?"

Bill zipped up, chuckling humorlessly. "You're the last man on earth to lecture somebody about priorities. Who was pissin' their pants in a corner while Ryan and I were bug wrestling?"

Hobbs said nothing.

"And when your little space engine blew a gasket, how many white coats did you trample tryin' to be the first one out Taggart Labs' front door?"

The man grabbed hold of his tie and wiped it across his damp forehead, but remained silent.

Bill wondered if he would turn on his television a month or so from now to find Ken Hobbs sweating again, only this time it would be behind a microphone with a lawyer at his side. This disaster would spark a media frenzy—

finger pointing, political grandstanding, investigations. Those directly responsible might be dead, but Bill had no doubt someone would be made to pay. The victims' families would demand it.

He thought of little Hannah sitting in the Liberty, her father's savaged body back at the bookstore, and picked up his rifle. "Let's go."

The metal plate that covered the tanks was next to a payphone at the edge of the lot. Hobbs walked over to the phone, put the receiver to his ear, then dropped it, letting it hang from its cord in the breeze.

"Line dead?" Bill asked, knowing it would be. Just like the phones at the county lock-up and the bookstore.

"Yes," Hobbs replied, clearly frustrated. "The quake must've cut the fiber optics."

Bill slid his prybar under the lip of the plate, smelling gasoline. "Give me a hand with this."

When Hobbs put his weight on the end of the bar, Bill set his rifle on the ground and used his hands to push the plate up and over. It landed with a loud clang, releasing strong fumes from the tanks below. Bill knelt down, lowered tubing through the opening, and siphoned fuel into the can. The sound was like rain on a tin roof.

"Here." Bill handed the full container up to Hobbs. "Put this in the Jeep and get your ass back here."

"For what?"

"There's no more than two gallons there. The way SUV's suck up gas, we'll be lucky to get anywhere with that."

Hobbs sighed, then looked around nervously, gas sloshing in the can as he rushed across the vacant lot. After a moment beside the Liberty, he hurried back with a silent container for Bill to refill.

An ear-piercing whistle blared.

They looked up and saw a creature—Deinonychus?—staring back at them from the convenience store roof. The wind blew through its brightly colored feathers, creating waves in a sea of paint, and its clawed toes hooked over the edge as if it were ready to pounce.

Bill felt his heart sprint within his chest. His eyes went to the rifle, but he knew he couldn't fire it without sparking gasoline vapors.

"Don't move," Hobbs whispered over the patter of the filling can. "I've seen *Jurassic Park* a dozen times. Dinosaurs can't see you if you don't move."

The creature's head twitched as it eyed them from its perch.

"Then why is it looking right at us?" Bill asked through clinched teeth.

Before Hobbs could offer an explanation, the animal leapt fifteen feet from the roof down to the blacktop. It leaned forward, chirping, its head tilting curiously from one side to the other. The feathers on its neck lifted slightly, then fell back into place. It continued watching them, nostrils flaring, tail swinging, sickle claw twitching, but it did not charge.

"It's the gas," Bill theorized. "I think the smell's got it confused."

Behind them, the Liberty's engine started up.

The creature's head snapped toward this new sound, the fan of feathers around its neck now flipping to full attention. It uttered a low, guttural growl, and its fingers danced.

"Hobbs, when I count to three, run like hell." Bill grabbed the rifle and rose to his feet. "One...two..."

Deinonychus sprang forward on its powerful legs, landing on Hobbs, knocking him down. He screamed and crossed his arms over his face. The animal bit cleanly through them.

Bill turned and ran, Hobbs' dying screams following him all the way to the Jeep. He climbed into the passenger's seat, and Ryan hit the gas before his door was even closed.

Another deinonychus was coming right at them. Bill had never seen an animal charge a speeding vehicle head on, but that's exactly what it did. It leapt onto the hood, a rainbow plume with claws and teeth, lost its footing, tumbled over the roof, then fell off the back end.

Shocked by the impact, Ryan instinctively stood on the brake and the anti-locks grabbed hold, bringing the Liberty to a jerky stop.

Whistling filled the air as more of the creatures rushed

them, pouncing on the Jeep as if it were living prey. Bill didn't know where they all came from, they seemed to be everywhere at once. They scratched at the metal, a sound worse than nails on chalkboard, and he could hear pops as those long claws punctured the body. The cab rocked on its axels, and for a horrible moment, he thought they would tip it over.

One of the animal's down-covered faces pressed against Bill's window, sliming it with drool.

"Feathered fuck!" He put the barrel of his rifle to its eye and shot through the glass, watching as the creature fell away in a crimson cloud.

Ryan floored the gas pedal and the Liberty lurched forward. Unable to hang on, the creatures rolled across the asphalt, growing small in the rearview mirror, their high-pitched whistles fading.

There was a low rumble, like rolling thunder, and the ground trembled beneath the tires. Ryan did his best to maintain control of the wheel. "Another earthquake."

"Mommy," Hanna called out, pointing, "what are those?"

When Bill followed her finger to the rear window, he saw creatures the size of Greyhound buses charging up the road. Small heads rode serpentine necks, and long tails swung behind them like wrecking balls on chains, damaging the brick and stucco walls that lined the street on either side. Their wrinkled skin was tiger-striped, and what appeared to be elongated porcupine quills lined their backs. One of the few dinosaur names Bill knew was brontosaurus. If he had to call them anything, that would have been it.

Ryan had another name for them. "Amargasaurus," he

said, staring wide-eyed into his mirrors. He sounded excited. "I don't believe it."

That made them pretty even. Bill stopped believing anything when he was tossed from his bunk.

As these new giants stampeded around the Jeep, Ryan tried to steer between them. It was amazing how fast they could run. With their enormous size, Bill would have thought their sheer weight would make them slow and lumbering, but they ran like the startled giraffe he'd seen in Discovery Channel videos.

Before Bill could even ponder what these beasts were running from, one of them crossed into the Liberty's path, causing Ryan to slam on his brakes again. The animals behind them knew nothing of brake lights. They plowed into the Jeep at full gait.

Ryan had not fastened his seatbelt when he moved to the driver's seat. He was thrown forward, smashing head first through the windshield. One of the giants then whacked the side of the Liberty with its whip-like tail, and the vehicle rolled right over him.

Bill watched the world spin by. He felt the sting of broken glass on his cheeks and forehead, felt pain in his shoulder and abdomen as his seatbelt grabbed him, threw him back against the seat, then felt the sudden embrace of a billowing airbag. When he opened his eyes again, he was dizzy, as if he had just stepped off the teacups at Disneyland, but even with this continued sense of rolling, he knew the Liberty had come to a stop.

Once he was oriented, Bill realized the Jeep was resting on its side. He heard Kim, Hannah, and Sarah crying, and turned to find them hanging from their belts in the back seat. Bill got himself unfastened, felt around until he found his rifle, then helped the women from their restraints.

They staggered from the wreckage together, but Kim quickly fell behind. She stopped in the middle of the road, screaming out for Ryan. A shadow came over her, and before Bill could shout a word of warning, the bolting amargasaurus stepped down, one hundred tons smashing her frail frame. When the giant took another stride, she remained stuck to the sole of its foot, her body going up into the air, limp arms flailing, then plunged back down to the asphalt. On its third step, she stayed on the pavement and the behemoth dashed on without her.

Bill pushed Sarah and Hannah toward the brick facade of an apartment building, holding them there. When the stampede finally passed them by, he heard a sound like barking in the distance and looked up in time to see the last amargasaurus disappear from view.

It looked as if it were falling.

After a few minutes, he took Hannah in his arms and yanked Sarah to her feet. "Come on," he told her.

She protested at first, but was soon walking quietly at his side. She wanted to leave this place just as badly as he did, even if it meant on foot.

Bill noticed the buildings on either side of the street were incomplete. At first, he thought the quake had toppled them, but he saw no rubble. The edges were clean, the structures chopped neatly in half. Even the street was broken here, becoming a road quite literally to nowhere, as if whatever had scissored through the buildings had cut away the rest of the world. He handed Hannah back to her mother and stepped up to the edge of this drop.

It was impossible.

Where the street ended, a steep rock face descended beneath a green canopy of palm trees. Bill could see sawed off sewer pipes and conduits of cable, all made level with the face of the sheer wall. He saw the herd of amargasaurus down there. They were all dead. Unable to halt their charge, they had run right off the cliff and were crushed under their own massive weight. They lay on a bed of cars and semi trucks that had preceded them over the edge. Some of these vehicles were still burning.

Bill's eyes rose to the horizon. Beyond the smoke from the wrecks below, he could see nothing but jungle and distant mountains. Some giant had scooped the entire city out of the ground and then dropped it in the middle of the Amazon.

The terrible truth struck Bill's brain like an arrow. Dinosaurs hadn't been caught in Einstein's Slingshot...*they* had. Kim told them her cell phone read "No Service." Bill now had to chuckle at that. There wouldn't be service for another 144 million years.

He sat on the end of the road, letting his legs drape over the edge of the broken asphalt. A dragonfly the size of an eagle hovered in front of him for a moment, then resumed its flight. He watched it spiral down onto a dead animal below.

Sarah looked out on the vista and fell to her knees. She hugged her daughter a little tighter, tears returning to her eyes, following tracks laid by the countless others that had proceeded them.

"Don't cry, Mommy," Hannah told her. She wiped at her mother's cheeks, then pointed to the flying things that circled overhead. "Look, see the baby dragons."

Ryan might have known what the winged creatures really were, but Bill didn't have a clue. A few of them landed and picked poor Kim's body apart, fighting each other for the tastiest morsels, their snouts made rosy and slick with her blood. One of the animals took flight with her arm clutched between its teeth. Bill saw her wristwatch glinting in the dying sunlight as it flew off.

*Looks like she had more meat on her bones than I thought.*

He turned away, looking at Sarah. "Tomorrow morning, we'll climb down into the forest," he told her, trying to be comforting, to get her to stop sobbing before something out there came to investigate. "There's gotta be others who made it. There's gotta be."

Bill thought of future paleontologists like Ryan, imagined them finding his fossilized remains next to cave paintings of dinosaurs climbing telephone poles and attacking Jeeps. He wondered what they would think of that, then smiled hopelessly.

Teakettle whistles blared. They were loud, close. If Bill shut his eyes, he could see the pack circling them, their sickle claws calling out for more blood.

He rolled the rifle's remaining shells between his fingers and palm, counting them over and over. One... two...three.

Just enough.

It was getting very dark now. Bill wanted to believe they would see the sun again. He really did.

# GOD LIKE ME

"We are experiencing isolated network problems. More details in fifteen minutes."

Dylan Mercer jumped at the distorted announcement that blared from a speaker in the ceiling above his head. Despite fifteen years of servitude to the company, he had yet to meet the owner of this voice of doom, but the tone was unmistakably female and it carried with it boredom and frustration in equal measure. He knew what she felt all too well. Just getting up in the morning, day after endless day, knowing the drudgery of this cubical awaited him, was sometimes more than he could bear.

The phone on his desk rang and Dylan answered it, the scripted words flowing instinctively from his mouth. "Thank you for calling Serra Industries, Dylan Mercer speaking, how may I assist you today?"

"Why the hell can't you manage to empty the fucking dishwasher in the morning?"

It was his wife. The line was "recorded for quality control" (meaning Big Brother was always listening, waiting for him to screw up), but Miranda didn't give a shit who heard her daily rants.

Dylan forced his voice to sound pleasant. "I'm sorry, sweetie. Hey, can I call you back in a few minutes on my lunch break?"

She went on as if he'd said nothing, "You expect me to do everything around here!"

The truth of the matter was that he would do cartwheels if she would lift a finger to do *anything* around their home. Her only job was to rest her bulk and keep the couch from flying away. There she would gorge on Little Debbie cakes and watch her daily dose of Montel, Oprah, and Springer sprinkled with soap operas. Occasionally, she would gain the strength to rise and go shopping with his money—money that never seemed to be enough to pay off the credit cards she filled.

The coffee in Dylan's Serra Industries mug began to boil. It sat in the middle of his desk on a napkin, but it steamed and bubbled just the same. Dylan didn't notice. He was too busy staring at the ceiling, wondering why he had married her, wondering why he was stuck in a life that was on the bullet train to oblivion. How much of it was of his own making?— the result of his own meek nature?

"I'm really busy, hon," he told her, trying to maintain his level tone. "Can I call you back about this?"

"You're worthless," she yelled and was gone.

Dylan slapped the phone onto the receiver and the dark liquid in his mug grew still again. He returned his focus to the spreadsheet that filled his computer screen. Absently, he reached for his pen and it rolled across the counter to meet his fingers like a puppy summoned by its master.

"Mercer."

Dylan's heart skipped a beat and he turned in the direction

of the voice, seeing Mr. Skellern, his supervisor. He was a small man; taller than a dwarf, but short enough to be called such behind his back. The man's hair could not even stand him, having abandoned his head at the earliest opportunity.

"Do you have the Korean sales figures?" the bald dwarf asked.

"Oh, yes." Dylan pointed at the numbers on his screen. "I have them right here."

"Then why don't I have them?" Skellern asked.

He opened his mouth to give an excuse, but he was denied the power of speech.

Skellern shook his shiny head. "If you can't handle the job to which you've been assigned, Mr. Mercer, I'll be forced to find someone who can." He started to walk away. "I'm sure you don't want that."

Dylan's hand made a fist at his side. *Idiot*, his mind muttered.

Skellern turned. "What did you say?"

He froze. Had he said it aloud? No. He was certain he hadn't spoken, yet his angry remark had been heard just the same.

"My office," Skellern snapped. "Now."

---

The desk that stood between them was huge, wooden, and unspeakably neat. Pictures stared at Dylan from gilded frames positioned on its lacquered surface with meticulous precision. There was the dark-haired trophy wife, the bald man shaking hands with celebrity-standing close to the stars of sport and screen as if to become popular by association, and even the slobbering image of the master's faithful Great Dane. On the wall behind the desk hung the parchments of academia, taunting Dylan with their calligraphy. *Skellern*, they said, *is most assuredly greater than you will ever be.*

"I'm concerned, Mr. Mercer." The words from his lips were comforting, but his eyes spoke a different language. "At Serra Industries, we try to provide an environment where you can grow and use your abilities to the best of their potential. But your work...let's just say it hasn't been your best as of late. In fact, it's been down right sloppy. Frankly, I don't know what to do with you. You're consistently late or calling in...and when you are here, you do nothing but complain about this company and your situation."

As he listened to Skellern speak, Dylan's hatred of the man deepened until there was no bottom to it. Of course *he* had nothing to complain about. What did this man know of work? He'd married the owner's daughter. He'd been born into that designer suit, born into that chair, and nursed by the board of directors. He'd never had to drive himself to work in the morning rush. He'd never done time chained to a computer in a prison cell masquerading as a workstation.

"Of course, I don't think any of what I'm saying should come as a shock to you. I don't know what is going on in your personal life——"

Like this little man cared what Dylan did when he was not on his clock.

"Are you listening, Mr. Mercer?"

Dylan nodded absently and Skellern droned on.

"If you need to take a leave of absence, clear your head of outside distractions, it's possible that we could work something out. But while you are here, Mr. Mercer, your co-workers expect you to pick up your slack. They expect it, I expect it, and our CEO Joel Serra expects it."

*Joel Serra doesn't have a heart*, Dylan thought.

Dylan pictured Mr. Serra on his annual Aspen ski vacation, pictured his heart exploding in his chest as he snaked his way down the slope. The force of the imagined blast turned the old man's ribcage to shrapnel that tore through his flesh and parka. In the vision, Serra fell face-first into a drift of fresh powder, draining blood and bile granting it the appearance of a huge cherry snow cone. The mental picture brought a grin to Dylan's face.

"If you proceed further down this current road," Skellern went on, "I'll have no choice but to respond with disciplinary action."

*If I were in charge,* Dylan thought, *it's* you *who would see disciplinary action.*

Skellern gave his head a shake, trying to play the disappointed father. "I'm sure you don't want that."

*If I had the power, you'd be fired!*

Without warning, the office door opened and Skellern's young secretary entered the room. "Sorry to bother you, sir, but there's an urgent call from the Aspen office—something about Mr. Serra being involved in an accident."

"Put it through, Miss Walsh."

She nodded and left the room, closing the door behind her.

A moment later, the phone rang on Skellern's desk. He looked up at Dylan as he reached for it. "Now you'd better get going," he said curtly. "Your remark has already cost you quite a bit of your lunch hour."

Dylan ground his teeth. *Fired!*

Skellern flew out of his chair and against the wall with tremendous force, shattering the glass covering his diplomas and certificates of merit. His face glowed with an inner light, as if the veins beneath were pumping phosphorus paint rather than blood. He opened his mouth to scream, and belched smoke and tongues of flame instead. Fire flared in his hair and spread out across his expensive suit, turning Skellern into a human torch.

Dylan was on his feet, staring at the blaze, knowing he had somehow ignited it. As preposterous as that concept was, it had so much allure that Dylan could not shake it. The flames set off the sprinkler in the office ceiling and an artificial rain soaked him. His mind resurrected a long dead memory from his childhood, a buried vision of toys dancing by themselves, followed closely by the forgotten recollection of his mother scolding him.

"They'll take you away from me," she'd warned. "They'll lock you in a room somewhere and run tests on you and you'll never see your family again."

The fire alarm was blaring in his ears. Dylan wished he could shut it off and his wish was granted. Behind him, the door opened. Someone was coming in. With a glance, he slammed it closed again—sending Skellern's secretary flying back against her desk. He walked over to the body of his former supervisor, watching the flames die beneath the downpour, and tried to think.

He'd killed a man just now—if you could call Skellern a man—and he'd done it with a simple thought. They would take him away now, just as his mother had promised. What could he do? What could he...

Dylan paused a moment in his panic.

What *could* he do?

He had no idea. His dread and guilt waned, replaced by sudden anger. He thought of a life that might have been and felt cheated. All his days, people had slighted him, laughed at his misfortune. His entire miserable existence, he'd been a pawn, an obedient lapdog wanting approval from one master or another. And yet, it had been he who should have been master. At this simple realization, a smile dawned on his lips—

the excited grin of a child. He'd just been given a new toy and longed to see what it could do.

The door opened again.

This time, he allowed it.

"What's going on in here?"

Barbie Walsh came back into the room, her eyes and voice filled with concern. She was wet from the indoor rain, her clothes clinging seductively to her figure. Her dark hair was matted to her head like a black hood. Her skin was tanned and glistening.

"Come to me," Dylan urged and was mildly shocked to find her move toward him without hesitation.

"What's going on?" she repeated meekly.

Dylan smiled. "I've always preferred blondes."

Her hair was eager to please him. The brown was leeched from it, washed away by the drizzle from the sprinklers above.

And he *was* pleased. This was the kind of woman he should have been with, the wife he should have had instead of Miranda. How Dylan wished he'd invoked these powers in high school and college. All those lonely nights could have been filled with passion; all those laughing women could have been forever silenced. "Kiss me."

There was an odd look in her eye, a questioning glance, but she did as he wished. Her lips were full, her tongue soft.

*What would Miranda say if she could see us like this?*

That odd feeling of guilt crept in again and Barbie broke the kiss. She took a step back, wiped her lips and slapped Dylan hard across the face. She might have been crying, but the tears were lost to the man-made rain.

"Security is on their way," she told him, her voice quivering. "When they get here, I hope they—"

Something on the floor behind the desk caught her eye, a

smoldering shape that had once been a man. She took two steps toward it.

"Mr. Skellern?"

"Don't look at him," Dylan commanded, the anger returning. "Look at me!"

Her eyes rushed back to him, but her body had received no order. It continued to face the desk as her head spun farther than anatomy would grant. Her spine ground the cartilage of her neck to pulp, her tendons snapped, her esophagus knotted. She was dead before she hit the floor, her belly and the back of her head against the soaked carpet, her lifeless eyes still on Dylan.

His stomach sank. For decades this power had been building within him untapped. *I've got to learn better control,* he thought as he backed away from what he had created. *I've got to focus.*

"Hold it!"

He whirled around to see the security guard in the doorway. The man's gun was drawn and his eyes alternated between Barbie's twisted body and Dylan.

Dylan's heart thudded wildly in his chest. This is what his mother had warned him about. This is why he'd made himself forget his own power. They would arrest him now. They would take him away and stick him in some lab in the basement of the Pentagon. They would...

*They can't do anything I don't let them do.*

Dylan blinked. Could that be right? Could he be that powerful? It was time to practice his control. He looked at the rent-a-cop's handgun. "Very scary," he told the man, "But not scary enough."

The skin on the guard's trigger hand burst open, muscle fibers coming unraveled from the bone. Cords of naked ligament wrapped around the 9mm pistol like the glistening tentacles of a squid, flesh flowing over the metal until it became a new, deadly paw. The man's face was flayed open beneath Dylan's direction, transformed into a screaming skull. Teeth grew outward to form tusks and winding filaments of bone created a mane of thorns across the man's meaty scalp. The guard-thing howled on and on, a string of rose-tinted drool hanging from its bony jaw. Dylan was pleased with the transformation, with the discipline he'd used to perform it.

He had the hang of it now.

Dylan looked up at the sprinkler heads and their shower immediately ceased. He walked calmly out of the office and into a flowing river of workers. With the drone of the fire alarm silenced, they were returning to their cubicles like bees to their honeycombs—all of their energy and lives spent toiling for the benefit and wealth of others. He was thankful he would no longer be one of them. No, he now had something far grander in mind for his life.

When Dylan reached the nearest stairwell door, he opened it and left Serra Industries behind.

---

The sun shone brightly as Dylan drove Skellern's black BMW convertible down the highway. It was the kind of car he had always wanted, the kind he had never been able to afford as a lowly sales consultant. When he'd seen it sitting in its reserved VIP spot, he simply touched the door and it opened for him willingly. At the thought of driving it, the engine purred, and now, as Dylan pressed the gas pedal to the floor, it roared.

He reached out with his mind and the slower traffic in his path parted like the Red Sea to his will. Cars flew and tumbled away in all directions as if blown from the road by hurricane winds, or wiped aside by the invisible hand of God.

*I am a god!* Dylan laughed as a Dodge Caravan was flung out of his way and into a Saturn coupe on his right. Both exploded in a ball of flame. *I have power over time and space, flesh and bone, life and death!*

Some of the cars ahead of him were now pulling over without his direction. They feared him. That was good. People worshipped what they feared. This was everything he'd ever wanted, everything he'd ever dreamed of as he sat drowning in the boredom of his workstation.

As Dylan grew closer and closer to his home, the smile on his face widened. "Oh dear, sweet Miranda," he said aloud. "Things are going to be very different around here from now on."

---

"What are *you* doing home?" she mumbled from the couch as he walked in the door. Her mouth was full.

"It's so wonderful, sweetie." Dylan took off his tie and flung it at her. It landed on her belly and slid onto the floor like a dead snake. "I'm so alive right now. It's almost like being reborn into another life—a *better* life."

Miranda hit the power button on her remote, silencing Oprah. "What the hell are you talking about? Why aren't you at work?"

"I quit."

The expression of utter shock on her face was hilarious, better than any he could have made for her if he had chosen to do so. After one failed attempt, she managed to lift herself from the cushions. She wore a large housedress that resembled a circus tent. She had not bothered to apply any make-up, and her hair was a wild, unkempt mane. *No*, he thought, *there's not enough magic in the world to make Miranda beautiful.*

"Dylan Mercer," she scolded, "this had better be a joke."

His reply was a sly grin. He turned away from her and walked into the kitchen. The fridge opened its door and spat out a beer. Dylan caught it and popped the top, foam cascading over his fingers onto the wooden flooring. Could he turn all the rivers to beer? Something told him that, if he really wanted to, he could do just that.

"*Don't you turn away from me,*" she screamed after him. "You go right back there and you *beg* for them to give you your job back."

"Sweetie," he said, "it's you who should beg."

Miranda fell to her knees with a thud that shook the entire room. Dylan could not help but chuckle at the sight. All his married days, he felt as if he had been living in a minefield— aware that the slightest wrong move would set her off and never sure of what those moves were until it was too late. Now, to see this ogre fall, to see her kneeling before him as if to pray, was truly priceless.

"You're such a bastard," she told him, rage bubbling up through the brown tar of her eyes. "Get your ass over here and help me up."

"Help you?" Dylan's chuckle became full-blown laughter. "Sure, Sweetie. Sure. Let me help you."

He reached out to her with his mind, mental fingers curling around her bulk and slightly pressing. Miranda's eyes widened at the sensation of pressure she felt against her abdomen. When he let go of her, Dylan heard her wheeze as she drew in rapid breaths.

"Call 911," she coughed. "You see what you've done? I'm...I'm having a heart attack!"

"Beg me to let you live."

The rage in her eyes bled into her face, making it red with fury. "Have you lost your mind?"

Dylan took a sip of his beer. "I'd say I was thinking clearly for the first time. You have no idea the power I have, Miranda. All these years, you've called me worthless, and spineless, and—"

"You *are* worthless!" she roared. "I ask you to—"

Dylan slammed his can down on the counter. "Don't interrupt me, bitch!"

"What did you call me, you miserable shit?" She actually tried to rise up and come at him, but he held her down with greater determination.

"You need to learn your place now, Miranda. There's a new pecking order in the Mercer household. From now on—"

"I hate you!" she howled.

"What did I say about interruptions?"

Miranda's tongue was yanked from her mouth by unseen hands, tearing loose from her gullet with a wet snap. She covered her lips with her hands and blood poured freely between her closed fingers. She tried to scream, but all she could muster was a sickly moan.

Dylan walked out from behind the counter and crouched in front of his wife. Miranda's tongue was on the carpet. He picked it up and held it out for her inspection. "Since you can't hold your tongue, I'll have to do it for you."

She took her hands from her mouth and hooked her bloody fingers into claws, as if to repay his actions by scratching out his eyes.

Dylan's mind grabbed her again, squeezing much harder than it had before. "All this time, it's *you* who've been worthless." He looked into her eyes as they bulged. "All this time, it was you who should have feared *me*."

*Thinner*, he thought. *I want her to be thinner.*

And now, as he continued to squeeze, he could see that she *did* fear him. Only now, as her sternum splintered and her hips cracked, did she fully understand just how powerful he was.

*Thinner*, he wished.

When Miranda screamed, it was a symphony to Dylan's ears. For once, these were not screams of anger. These were cries of joyous agony. Her belly ruptured and her bowls unspooled, and still she screamed. The air filled with a bloody mist as her bones continued to fracture and puncture her flesh, and still she screamed. Her stomach rose until she vomited it, and her screaming stopped.

Dylan kept squeezing, however. *Thinner*, he wished again. Thinner.

Flesh and bone continued to tear and break, compacting, becoming more and more slender. Blood was wrung from her form like water from a dishrag. Finally, when her skull caved and her eyes ruptured, when she was reduced to a steaming, oozing sac of flesh, he released her and she fell to the carpet with a sick thud.

Dylan was breathing heavily. He stood over Miranda's remains and shook his head. She had been useless to him. She could never have been his goddess. He needed a new and improved Miranda to rule by his side—a beautiful Miranda that appreciated him and his power.

As he thought this, the blood that welled up from his wife's ruined carcass frothed and bubbled. It slowly solidified, forming a fleshy cocoon laced with veins. Dylan watched in awe as the sack inflated with bone, sinew, and skin until a delicate hand pushed through its membrane. A newly formed human being stepped free of the chrysalis—a woman. Her hair was woven in flaxen braids and her body was toned and bronzed. Her eyes were the color of clear sky and her full, pouting lips were moist and wanton.

Dylan's mouth fell open in disbelief. He looked at this

woman, clasping her hand in his without touch, bringing his creation closer for inspection. She was the most beautiful thing he had ever seen—his woman, his goddess.

"We need to get away from here," he told her, looking around the drab, worn house on which he paid not one but two mortgages. "This is not a place fit for us. A god and goddess should have a palace on a high mountain from which to rule."

He remembered paintings he'd seen of Zeus on Mount Olympus and the ground quaked beneath his feet. The walls of his ranch home crumbled as stone pillars and marble facades seemed to sprout from the very earth. Dylan had the sensation of being in an elevator that was rapidly climbing. He looked through developing stone archways and saw clouds falling by, then closed his eyes—visualizing a mountain that grew until it surpassed the height of Everest, grew until its summit nearly sliced open the bubble of atmosphere surrounding the Earth. And then, as suddenly as it began, the eruption stopped.

When he opened his eyes again, Dylan saw that he was standing in the great hall of a palace of marble and gold that sparkled in the failing sunlight. At the far end, a stone staircase led to a pair of jeweled thrones. Dylan was pleased with what he had forged. He led his new bride up the steps and they took their seats. "This," he said as he caressed the armrests, "is truly a dwelling fit for the king and queen of the world."

His bride nodded her agreement, but said nothing.

Now that he had the power of creation, Dylan had no need for the beings that crawled across the face of the earth below. They knew the old Dylan Mercer, the meek and mild Dylan Mercer who had been afraid of his own shadow. They would never accept him as all-powerful. They would never willingly serve him. "The old god so hated the world that He washed it away and started fresh, filling it with those who would worship Him. I'll do the same, only better. What He cleansed by flood, I'll purge by flame."

With that simple proclamation, he envisioned dormant computers spitting launch codes into every missile silo across the globe. He saw rockets scream to life, thrusting from forgotten burrows on blazing shafts of glowing smoke. In his mind, he watched them arc across the heavens, guided by chips no larger than a thumbnail while atomic reactions within their silky warheads lay slumbering in dreams of light and dissolution.

Dylan smiled. "Soon, the Earth will die and be reborn from its ashes like a mighty phoenix. Then my work will——"

He never finished his sentence.

The pointed warhead of an Intercontinental Ballistic Missile burst through the marble wall above his thrown, the wall he had erected in the path of its trajectory. Dylan watched a rain of heavy debris fall toward him. Before he could think to wish it away, a great chunk of stone slammed into his face. His skull shattered like fine china, his powerful brain was crushed to pulp, and far below, the world he so despised was purified in the nuclear fire.

# TO KNOW HOW TO SEE

Something was wrong with Lee's face. A small comet passed the *Ambrosia*'s cockpit window, and Sean Corbett saw its streaking tail reflect off the man's skin, shimmering across his cheek and forehead, across the bridge of his nose, as if they were the sculpted features of a wax mask instead of true flesh.

Lee's glassy eyes lifted from the electronic book he'd been reading for the past hour. "What's the matter?"

The comet vanished as suddenly as it had appeared, leaving the cramped chamber dimly lit by the soft glow of monitors and LEDs that littered its consoles. Sean rubbed his eyes, convincing himself it had been a trick of the light. "Nothing, sorry."

Lee shook his head, muttering something under his breath as he resumed his studies.

Sean continued work on the instrumentation checklist, making notes with a pen clutched in metallic fingers. While drilling on Titan six years ago, a rockslide crushed his right arm. At first, he'd been unable to pick up a glass without shattering it, or use the bathroom without crying out in pain, but after six months of physical therapy, and years of experience, he could now perform even the most delicate of tasks. There was no feeling in the prosthesis itself, but this morning, he awoke to find his shoulder throbbing—a dull, deep pain, like a toothache. He chalked it up to a pulled muscle, downed a few painkillers, and went on about his duties.

Though it was now his shift in the pilot's seat, there was very little for Sean to do. *Ambrosia* took the reins as soon as they cleared the asteroid belt. She would need a human touch when they approached Nautilus station, but for now, their ten-member crew simply took turns babysitting her systems.

After a few minutes, Sean's attention returned cautiously to the man sitting next to him, examining his skin once more, finding it pale...shiny, without a single hair or blemish. It just didn't look *real*.

"You okay?" Lee asked. The skin above his left eye tore as he spoke, split like rubber stretched thin.

Sean's eyes widened. His mouth fell open in stunned silence.

"What's wrong?" Lee turned his head toward the cockpit window, as if expecting to see some stellar phenomenon occurring behind him. Finding nothing of interest, he turned back to Sean, the rip in his forehead now larger—a gaping, bloodless wound that ran from his hairline to his eyebrow.

Something moved in that darkness.

Sean squinted, trying to see what it was. Peering into Lee's torn forehead was like looking through a crack in a raven's egg. He saw shifting, flapping bits of strange anatomy that were far from human.

Panic flooded Sean's brain as he realized he was being watched. The thing beneath Lee's façade had trained its hidden eyes upon him. Did it know that its disguise had been compromised? Was it looking for signs that Sean was aware of its existence?

He turned, focused on the instrument panel for a moment. The tiny space suddenly felt even more confined. His galloping heart demanded more oxygen, but there seemed to be none left in the control room. He had to get out of there.

"I think I'm gonna be sick," Sean said aloud, and it was the truth. He glanced at the hatch behind them. It seemed so far away. "I have to...I gotta go see the doc."

The Lee-thing nodded. "Okay, man. Need me to walk you down there?"

"No!" Sean said too quickly. He felt a blast of air from an overhead vent. His skin was now slick with sweat. "I can make it."

With deliberate calm, he rose, managed to squeeze between the seats without touching the imposter, then took a backward step toward the exit. His left hand shook, but his prosthesis was cool and steady. He pressed a green-lit button to open the hatch and ducked as he stepped quickly into the narrow corridor beyond.

The Lee-thing stared at him.

"I'll see you later," it said.

Sean punched the button, closed the hatch, sealed the alien in. There was a fire alarm next to the door. For a moment, he considered breaking the glass, bringing the rest of his ship-mates to his aid. Instead, he ran for the Medlab, for Carla.

---

"Do you actually love me?" she asked.

The voice came across Sean's headset, each word punching a hole through the steady rattle of his own respiration. He twisted around, his heavy boots leaving marks in the obsidian dust. "What?"

Blue-white lights rimmed Carla's faceplate, making her pale, freckled features glow like a beacon in the darkness. She wasn't looking at him. Instead, she used the small keyboard sewn into the wrist of her environment suit, typing survey notes about the asteroid into her log. "I said—"

"I heard what you said. I just can't believe you'd even question it. Of course I love you."

Her brown eyes met his through the glass. "The computer could have picked another woman to be your partner on this trip, then you would've fallen for her instead of me."

"Not a chance."

A smile, but her voice remained serious, "You sound pretty sure about that."

"Carla...out of all the hundreds of women the company could have paired me with for these last two years, you were the *most* compatible. Computers don't lie."

Exhaust vapor erupted silently from the back of her helmet, crystallizing. "So this is love because a machine says it should be?"

"No, the machine said it would be because it is." He studied her, becoming mildly annoyed. Where was she going with this? "Look at the rest of the crew. Not every pairing turned into romance."

"So the computer was wrong about them, but it's right about us?"

"*Yes.*" Now frustrated, he glanced at the monitors on the robot drilling rig and saw that it had shattered a bit boring into the heavily cratered, rocky terrain. *Shit.* Sean quickly changed frequencies on his intercom. "Orpheus...stop."

The machine withdrew its smoking auger, the metal

glowing bright red, and its cameras stared back at them as if to question why they had not noticed sooner.

Sean flipped back to Carla's channel, then scaled the side of the rig. "I've got to change that."

"Need any help?"

He rotated the housing. In the cargo hold, he could hear it click when it moved into position, but out here, in this vacuum, he had to rely on feel. "I think I got it."

Carla nodded at his right shoulder. "Do you miss your real arm, the one you were born with?"

"When it first happened, yeah, sure I did." He climbed down to one of the seven support struts that extended from the sides and front of the rig, then hopped onto the surface, clouds of obsidian particulates billowing around his boots.

She took the decapitated bit from his hands and handed him a replacement. "If they could have given it back to you, would you have taken it?"

The memory of that day flashed in Sean's brain: coming to, being told that his arm had been ground to a pulp. He swallowed, trying to push it all back down. "That wasn't an option."

"But if it had been," she prodded, "would you have opted for reattachment, or for the mechanism?"

He snickered humorlessly. "At the time, I guess I would've been happy to get my real arm back."

"And now?"

Sean pulled himself back onto the rig with more ease than other men. "I'm sure there's a point to all this?"

Carla shrugged. "I was just thinking about how much we've given up for the sake of our respective careers, wondering if it's all been worth it. You lost your arm." She put the ruined drill bit into the tool chest at the back of the rig. "And I gave up my womb."

He paused for a moment, wondering if he should say something, not knowing any fitting words. Sterilization was mandatory for deep space travel. Simple mathematics. Air, food, water, and supplies had to be rationed, carefully calculated for a set number of people. Adding a baby into the equation, perhaps a year or two away from the nearest outpost or settlement, could put everyone's lives in jeopardy.

Carla asked, "Have you ever seen artificial gestation, been to one of the nurseries?"

Sean grunted, twisting the new part into place. "Can't say I have."

Her gloved hand raked the chest of her suit, her frustrated fingers unable to fiddle with the silver Saint Albert medallion and chain buried beneath the insulated fabric. Albertus Magnus, she'd told him, was the patron saint of scientists, her protector, and she never took it off, not even when she showered. "Picture row after row of glass tubes filled with oxygenated liquid, each one home to an embryo at a different stage of development. I saw parents smiling in on their unborn children, showing the still-forming fetuses off to friends and family. There was this adorable, curly-haired little girl. She tapped on the glass, the way kids used to do with aquariums." Carla raised her fist and acted it out. "Her father tried to get her to quit, but she just kept tapping and waving, trying to get that baby inside to open its eyes and look at her. Everyone was so happy, so proud, but it just left me feeling really sad and...cold, like something beautiful had been taken away in the name of progress."

Sean tightened a few bolts with his wrench. "That sounds odd, coming from a scientist."

Carla was silent for a moment, and he glanced down to see her searching for words, her lips parted, her eyes off to the side, then downcast, her hand still on her chest, trying to play with the hidden medallion and chain.

Finally, she said, "The scientist in me sees the gain, but the woman in me feels the loss. Our flesh and blood bodies have become disposable, *obsolete*. We give them up piece by piece without so much as a second thought. As soon as we discover a way to download our consciousness into a mainframe, everyone will opt to do it. True immortality."

"That wouldn't be you," he told her, "it'd be a copy."

"But it would be everything I know, which is everything that makes me me."

He slid his wrench back into his tool belt, then nodded at her wrist. "You can type everything you know into that log, and it wouldn't make it alive, just...thorough."

"Well, alive or not, people will do it in droves, just give it all up and stop being human altogether."

He climbed down from the rig to stand in front of her, rubbing his shoulder through the fabric of his suit. "Would *you* do it?"

Carla shrugged. "Probably not." Her eyes locked with his through the glass of their sealed faceplates. "I don't think I want to sacrifice anything else."

Sean took a step toward her. "What's going on?"

"The mission's almost over," she said, "and we'll have some tough decisions once we reach Nautilus, whether or not to renew our contracts, what we'll do if we don't sign up for another tour, where we'll—"

"You're thinking about leaving Nova Mining?"

Her face grew somber, and her eyes rose to the countless moons that drifted across the horizon. "It's certainly an option."

Medlab was free of the clutter that appeared throughout much of the ship. Doctor Edwards had music playing, relaxing orchestral tones. Four beds lined the far wall. They were empty now, but if there had been patients, Sean thought the music would have put them to sleep.

Carla was in a small corner she'd appropriated from the doctor, hunched over an ocular probe. Auburn curls spilled across the shoulders of her tan flight jacket, and her delicate fingers adjusted the controls, increasing magnification. The core samples Orpheus had mined were grouped on her glass tabletop. She analyzed each in turn, looking for a rich vein of ore.

Sean reached over and touched her arm, giving her a start.

"Jesus." Her jacket was unzipped, and she clutched at the white blouse beneath, pulling it tight across her breasts. "I thought you were on Bridge duty this morning?"

"I am...I was." His mind was still racing, incredible visions of concealed aliens being chased by rational, logical concerns about his own sanity.

Carla rolled her eyes, the Saint Albert medallion that hung from her neck rising and falling with her chest as she giggled. "Come to take me to lunch?"

*No, I've come to see if I'm losing my mind.*

He studied her eyes, her skin, the beauty mark just above her glossy red lips. He touched her cheek with his trembling left hand, felt its warmth, and knew she was very human.

She frowned. "Sean...Did something happen up there?"

"Have you seen Lee since we've been back on the ship?"

Carla shook her head and continued to look him over. "I don't think I've seen anyone but you and Doctor Edwards since we went through decon last night. Wasn't he up in the cockpit with you?"

"Yes, but..." Sean paused, deciding to be cautious until he

knew more. He extended his arm, took her soft hand in his metal fingers, and his shoulder flared with pain, igniting sparks within his eyes.

"It's still bothering you." She studied his prosthesis with concern.

"I'm fine."

"Liar. Look, while you're here, you should at least let Edwards take a look at it."

Sean glanced across the room, seeing the doctor's office in the opposite corner. Clear liquid ran down the glass walls that separated it from the rest of the lab, creating waterfalls that, like the music, were meant to calm those being treated.

"You're right," he told her. "I'll talk to the doc, see if he can help me."

"Good." Carla kissed his cheek, then grabbed two small display pads off the table—the most recent downloads of her technical journals. "I'll wait for you in the cafeteria."

She pulled away and Sean reluctantly let her go. He thought for a moment, then said, "If you see Lee, just...keep an eye on him. Don't get too close."

"Okay, you've officially scared the shit out of me. What—?"

"I'll explain it all over lunch."

Carla nodded, then disappeared down the corridor with her books.

Sean stepped over to stand in Edwards' doorway. The man had his back to him, studying a large monitor that filled the rear wall. "Knock-knock."

Edwards turned. His eyes lay hidden beneath a visor that allowed him to see temperature fluctuations, perform diagnostic scans, and be linked to the Medlab's computer. A red and blue patch on the breast of his lab coat labeled him the ship's chief medical officer—the ship's only medical officer, truth be told. He smiled, his lips surrounded by the stubble of a three-day-old beard. "Corbett. How's it going?"

"I was about to tell Carla something, but I thought I should run it by you to see what you thought first."

"I think I'm honored." A metal desk filled the center of the room. Edwards sat in the high-backed leather chair behind it, then motioned to a smaller seat nearby.

Sean went into the office, watching the Medlab entrance through watery glass; afraid Lee might walk in at any moment.

Edwards pressed a button on the edge of his desk, turning the smart glass opaque, preserving their privacy. "So, what's on your mind?"

"You'll think I'm a head case."

The doctor chuckled. "I already *know* you're a head case. We all are. We're pissing our lives away out here."

"Yeah." Sean offered up a laugh of his own, but it was a poor attempt, void of any real amusement. "Here's the thing...This is crazy, but I was just in the cockpit with Lee, and his face looked like a rubber mask. I saw it tear, saw something move around inside his head, like some kind of...some kind of *creature.*" He cringed as he spoke the word. "It was like Lee was just a costume this thing was wearing, a disguise, like it was spying on me. I could feel it looking at me, not with Lee's eyes, but with eyes *behind* his eyes."

They regarded each other a moment.

Edwards was first to break the silence, "That's the craziest Goddamned story I've ever heard in my life."

Sean's mouth went dry. "It looked so *real.*"

"Bullshit." The doctor pointed at him. "If you thought it was real, you would've gone on the com system, announced it to everyone instead of walking in here to talk to me. Besides, I sat across from Lee at breakfast this morning, and if he was some kind of alien, I think I would've noticed."

Sean ran his left hand over his mouth and chin. "So I've lost all my marbles, and Lee is just...Lee."

"Lee's fine," the doctor assured him.

"Thank God," Sean whispered, exhaling as if he had held his breath for a very long time.

"And you're not crazy," Edwards went on to say.

Sean raised his eyebrow.

"We both know what it takes to make it onto one of these flights," the doctor said. "You don't work for Nova or anybody else unless you've passed all the genetic and psychological testing."

He listened; relaxed a bit.

"Sean, did you know that if your great-great-aunt on your mother's side had the genetic marker for stuttering, you wouldn't be here right now."

He looked at the doctor.

Edwards nodded. "I'm serious."

Sean laughed, a nervous, relieved chuckle.

"I'd chalk it up to stress," the doctor told him, "but you can't be under any more stress than the rest of us. The damn ship runs itself. Something happen on that asteroid yesterday?"

"I don't know..." Sean shrugged, feeling the dull throb in his shoulder become a stabbing pain. He winced. "I think I pulled a muscle working on the rig. Hurts like hell."

The doctor stood and walked over. He touched the side of his visor. "When did you first notice it?"

"This morning."

"*Before* you saw that monster in Lee's head?"

Sean nodded. Hearing the doctor say it like that...it sounded so ridiculous, so far-fetched.

Edwards hit his visor button again, switched to a different type of scan. "And you've had that prosthesis of yours for...what?—six years now?"

"Yeah." Sean had a sudden, frightening thought. Could the pain be a signal that, after all these years, his body was rejecting this foreign apparatus?

The doctor nodded and moved away, walked to the monitor on the back wall. Sean could see the man's face reflected in the screen. It looked somehow distorted, as if the glass was a funhouse mirror. "Besides your little fieldtrip with Carla, when was the last time you worked in natural gravity?"

"I don't know...six years ago, I guess. On Titan."

"Ahuh." He touched the screen, initiated a download from his visor into the system. Images strobed on the large monitor: bones, shadowy ribbons of tissue, bright bolts and wires where Sean's prosthesis had been attached to the sawed-off stump of his surviving right arm. "Well, I think I know what's causing your pain *and* your visions."

"Don't keep me in suspense, Doc. What is it?"

Edwards continued to study the screen. Sean could not make out the small text displayed there, but when the doctor spoke, it almost sounded as if he were reading it aloud. "Fifty years ago, when they perfected artificial gravity, medical officers discovered that prolonged exposure caused people to develop pressure-induced conditions, similar to what deep sea divers experienced on Earth when they were down too long. Today, the technology has been fine-tuned, and the disorder only occurs in a small percentage of people who live and work in space, but the symptoms are clear: manifests as pain in the joints, most commonly the shoulder. Can lead to hand tremors, claustrophobia, and...drum roll, please...delusions."

*That's why his reflection still looks so odd in the monitor glass,* Sean told himself.

Edwards went on, "We know what it is. We can treat it. Your world will be much less interesting very soon."

"So...what?—I just need to take a pill or something?"

"Years ago, they'd stick you in a hyperbaric chamber and let you decompress." The doctor snickered. It was a peculiar sound, distorted, hollow. "Today, all I have to do is give you an injection of Talavera."

Edwards turned away from the wall monitor and the blood left Sean's head. It had not been a trick of the glass. The doctor's face *had* changed. It was now a pale, lifeless masquerade, and just as in the cockpit, Sean could sense a presence behind that façade, appraising him.

"So, let's get you fixed up," it said, its speech a twisted impersonation of the doctor's distinctive voice.

Fear crawled through Sean, leaving an icy cold in its wake. Part of him was willing to believe this was all a mirage, a side effect of the condition Edwards had just described to him, but there was another voice in his head, the primal voice of instinct, of self preservation, and that voice was telling him this *thing* was not the doctor, and that he was now in very real danger.

Sean stood, fighting to maintain his composure. *This isn't real. This isn't real. This is—* "Great...great. I've got some things I need to take care of right now, but I'll come back later and we can—"

"Sit down, Sean. This'll just take a second." The creature opened a drawer in the wall beneath the monitor and reached inside, bringing something out into the light.

The object was shaped like a gun, but it wasn't constructed of metal, or plastic, or even ceramic. It appeared to be bone and corrugated tubing, covered over by a thin, gray membrane, a living thing with a latticework of black veins that pulsed and breathed. It was tapered, ending in a wrinkled sphincter that rhythmically constricted, then relaxed. A pink snake slithered out through this opening, an obscene tongue crowned with a long, barbed thorn.

"What the hell is that?" Sean asked, unable to stop himself.

"Just relax," the doctor-thing told him. He acted so calm, as if Sean shouldn't find anything odd about the writhing thing in his hand. "You won't feel a thing."

*It's a syringe,* Sean told himself. *That's all it is. Edwards isn't behaving strangely because he doesn't see what I see. He doesn't share my delusion. He doesn't—*

*He doesn't know you can see what it really is.*

The creature took a menacing step forward and Sean dove for it without thinking. He grabbed its camouflaged face in his robotic fingers, latched onto its wrist with his human hand, kept its fleshy weapon and alien stinger at bay. He pushed it back, crashed it into the wall monitor, shattered its skull beneath the force of his hydraulic grip. A black, viscous fluid spilled from its torn mask, oozing out between Sean's metal fingers like used motor oil.

He released his hold and backed away, staring at the remains with disgust. The Edwards-thing hung there on the wall, arms at its side, suspended by the jagged shards of monitor glass that dug into its ruined cranium.

While the alien was now dead, there was still life left in its vein-laced tool. The object fell from its master's dead grasp and landed with a *clang* on the metal flooring below. Its pink tongue whipped and writhed, its barb searching for a suitable target. Sean couldn't tell if it was an animal or a device, but when he stomped on it, grinding it beneath the tread of his boot, it let loose a shrill scream, like the bleating of a dying lamb.

Sean caught sight of his prosthesis, of his metal fingers covered in dark fluid, and the smell of freshly sheared copper assailed his nostrils, gagging him. He edged away from the body, took a few wobbly backward steps, and bumped into the desk. Sean gripped it like a drowning man latching onto a floatation device, his heart running a marathon as he frantically tried to assess his situation. He could not believe what had happened.

He'd just killed a man.

*No*, his mind corrected, *not a man.*

Sean shook his head at the absurdity of it all. He was sick, temporarily insane.

He forced himself to look at the weapon, to stretch out his human hand and actually feel its soft, slimy surface. It was like caressing an earthworm.

A pink tendril poked through the weapon's ruptured side.

Sean leapt back, pressed himself against the edge of the desk, and watched as a small squid-like animal crawled out onto the floor, a single black eye surrounded by writhing tentacles. He counted them, noting that there were seven, not eight or ten like the animals of Earth.

Seven.

Its cyclopean eye rolled from side to side, taking in its surroundings before coming to rest on Sean's shocked face.

It shot across the room, those odd-numbered tentacles propelling it, leaving behind a trail of mucus. Sean chased after it and slammed his foot down hard, tried to crush it like a roach, but it was too fast for him. It reached an air vent and slid through the grate into the ducts that catacombed the ship.

Sean suddenly wished he could talk this over with Doc Edwards, that he could hear the man tell him this was still all in his head, and then it hit him like a cold spray:

*The doc was going to inject that* thing *into my body.*

When Sean walked in, Edwards had been studying the crew's medical records. He didn't find anything odd about that at the time, but now it appeared the alien may have been researching their bodies, trying to make these copies as perfect as possible, or perhaps searching for reasons to call crew members in for an injection.

If that squid had entered Sean's body, what would have happened to him?

There was still so much he didn't know.

Sean glanced back at the ruined tool on the floor. Their technology appeared to be constructed of living tissue. If that was the case, then the squid may have been another kind of device, designed to tap into a human brain. Perhaps it could download memories as easily as the doctor's visor relayed images, memories that could be given to the alien who would later pose as Sean.

The vision of a beast in Sean's clothing walking up to Carla flashed in his mind, and he shuddered.

An extra lab coat hung on the wall beside the monitor. Sean used it to wipe the dark, sticky fluid from his prosthesis. When he was done, he tossed it to the floor, his face twisted in a grimace of repulsion.

A section of frosted glass slid open, then closed tight behind him. Sean realized he had to make sure that the door could not be re-opened, that no one else could get in to find the doctor's body. Acting quickly, he turned and put his metallic fist through the control panel. He saw a bright flash, felt a powerful jolt course through his body, and was thrown across the room. He landed near the hatch, his prosthesis smoking.

*Jesus, that was stupid.* Still dazed, Sean managed to roll onto his knees. He tried to reach out for one of the beds, but his metallic arm was now limp, useless, heavy. *Great. Just...fucking* brilliant.

Sean used his left hand to pull himself up, held onto the foot of the bed until the room stopped spinning, then staggered into the thin corridor beyond the hatch.

Sean ducked beneath a bulkhead, fear propelling him down the access tunnel. *Ambrosia*'s lower levels were like a maze of mineshafts, dimly lit by the miles of fiberoptic cable that lined the walls. The ceilings were low, and the corridors just wide enough for a single technician or repair droid to slide through. He slowed as he approached each intersection, afraid of what might be lurking around the next bend.

He was close to the engines now; could hear their steady drone, feel their vibrations in the metal of the flooring, the walls, even his prosthesis. The mechanical limb dangled at his right side, its dead weight pulling on his shoulder, sending waves of pain to soak the shores of his reeling brain. He clenched his teeth and wedged his way through an open hatch into the ship's hold.

The cargo area was a very tall hallway. A steady drip of condensation from coolant pipes left bumpy, reddish-brown patches of corrosion across its walls and floor. Overhead, supplies hung like stalactites from the high ceiling, suspended by a complex system of pulleys, wires, and chains.

Sean wasn't surprised to find Sanderson among these cartons and tools. The quartermaster occasionally bunked here in the ship's bowels. And the fact that Sanderson was not really Sanderson didn't shock him either. If these aliens took over when they were off the ship, it was likely Sean and Carla were the only two human beings left.

What Sean did find astonishing, however, was the speed in which he was able to identify this new imposter. With Lee and the doctor, it had taken some time to see through whatever hologram or cloak they used to make their suits appear more realistic, but he had known this one at first sight.

"Hey there," the Sanderson-thing said.

Sean raised his left hand and gave a slight wave of acknowledgement.

The weapons locker was on the opposite wall, on the other side of the alien. Looking at its face, Sean wondered if he could get away with this. Glass eyes, rubber skin. How was he supposed to pretend he didn't notice? It was going to realize he could see.

"Feeling better?" it wanted to know.

"Fine." Sean strained to put a pleasant smile on his face. "Why?"

It shrugged. "Lee said you were sick."

His grin slipped a bit. "Word spreads fast on this ship."

The thing said nothing, and Sean found himself wondering what it was doing there beneath its disguise. He looked down, studied the clipboard it held in its hand. It had been taking inventory, checking to see what types of equipment were stored here in the hold. If you asked the *real* Sanderson where something was, he would reach out and find it without even looking.

"Must've been something I ate." Sean forced himself to meet the alien's eyes. "You know how bad that re-hydrated pizza can be."

It stared at him for a moment, uncomprehending, then gave a lame chuckle. "Yeah...yeah, I do."

Sean nodded. *Sure you do.* "Anyway, I saw the doc and he gave me a shot, made me all better."

A hidden mechanism pulled at the mask's rubber lips, forming a satisfied smile that sent chills down Sean's spine.

*Now it thinks that squid's inside me,* he realized. *What was it supposed to do?*

"Glad to hear it." The Sanderson-thing turned away, going back about its business of cataloging human tools. "So what brings you down here?"

"Carla's missing a core sample. Just came to see if Orpheus still had them."

"Orpheus?"

"Yeah, the driller."

"Oh, right."

*It didn't know the name. It really didn't know.*

"Be my guest," the thing told him, pointing over its shoulder. "It's back there."

Sean took a deep breath and made steps toward the arms locker, keeping the creature in the corner of his eye as he passed by. Would it have one of those stingers with it? — Perhaps some other, more lethal bit of alien technology? If it did, it made no move to use them.

When he reached the locker's keypad, Sean entered his personal code to open the doors. No alarm would go off, but if they decided to run a report, it would show that he was the last to have access. They appeared to still be learning their way around the ship and its systems, however, so he doubted they would take the time.

"What are you doing?" the Sanderson-thing asked, its synthetic voice curious but stern.

Sean stopped. He glanced at the rock climbing equipment on the wall beside him, finding a blue-handled pickaxe. He reached for it, yanked it from its perch, and whirled around— driving the spike through this forgery's ear and skewering the alien within. The thing dropped to its knees, teetered a moment, then collapsed, the pickaxe handle rising like a blue monolith from the oil slick that poured across its rubber face and onto the floor.

*Two down,* Sean thought.

He turned back to the weapons trove; found it loaded with pulse rifles, 9mm handguns, and six drawers of seismic survey charges. A small pushcart sat empty nearby. Sean pulled it to him, filled it in a hurry.

Carla was waiting.

---

The cafeteria was small, dimly lit by tiny incandescent spots above each of its dozen tables. There had been a running joke among the crew that this lack of light was intentional, so they wouldn't have to see what they were eating. Each table was a gray metal mushroom, bolted to the floor and surrounded by swivel chairs.

Sean's gaze darted to the left.

Four doppelgangers in the room, two men and two women. Lee was among them. His face was now patched, that window to the squirming, flapping alien within closed up, but he still looked just as counterfeit as he had in the cockpit. The other man was meant to be Copeland, the women Fritz and Montgomery. Montgomery had been sitting with her back toward him, and Sean held the glimmer of hope that she might still be human...until she turned her head. These things were much better at replicating hair than human skin. They sat around their table, huddled over uneaten lunches, conversing in whispers.

Sean's eyes flew back to the right, finding Carla. She sat next to the food dispensers, just a few short meters away. He swallowed before entering, the cold metal of a hidden 9mm pistol against his abdomen, providing him comfort.

The hatch closed behind him with the sound of a striking cobra, attracting the Lee-thing's attention.

"Doc fix you up?" it asked.

Sean offered it a polite nod, then walked over to join Carla, trying his best to act nonchalant. Her tray was empty and she nursed a large cup of *Ambrosia*'s coffee as she read her technical journal.

"About time," she said as he sat down. "I thought you'd abandoned me." She looked him over and her eyes filled with concern. "You're still sweating. What did Edwards say?"

"I'm fine," he lied, wiping his brow with his left sleeve. It felt as if an angry swarm had landed on his right shoulder, each bee taking its turn at stinging him.

She lowered her book and her coffee, her voice uneasy. "Well, if you won't tell me the truth about that, at least tell me what the hell is going on with Lee."

"Have you looked at him?"

"Only for about the last twenty minutes."

Sean bobbed his head slightly in the creature's direction. "Look closer, the others too."

She started to turn around.

"Wait!" He whispered. "Don't be obvious about it."

Carla flashed a mixture of annoyance and bewilderment, then slowly turned her head, brushing a hand through her bright red locks, as if she were actually trying to see something in her hair.

*Slick. Very slick.*

When her eyes met his again they were still filled with confusion. "What?"

He bent over the table. No matter how quiet he tried to be, his voice still sounded as if it were echoing off the cafeteria's gray metallic walls. "You don't see it?"

She leaned in as well, speaking just as softly as he had been. "What is it that I'm supposed to see?"

"They're aliens."

Carla gaped at him. "They're *what?*"

"You heard me."

She laughed, but not for long. "You're serious."

He nodded, hoping his face conveyed just how grave the situation was.

"Jesus, Sean..." Her fingers found the medallion that hung from her neck, stroking Saint Albert's silver nose. "Have you told anyone else about this?"

"I told Doc Edwards, but he turned out to be one of *them*. He tried to inject me with this...this squid-like creature that—" He saw the look of shocked skepticism in her eyes. "I know how wild and paranoid it all sounds, okay, I do. I didn't want to believe it was true either. And if it was just my vision, I wouldn't have believed it, but I've felt smooth, slimy skin; smelled the black fluid they use for blood. This is real, God damn it!"

"Sean, I know you believe this, but just think for a moment..." She smothered Saint Albert with the palm of her hand. "If there are other intelligent beings out there some-where, and someday we make that first contact, they'll be explorers, just like us. They might try to signal us, meet with us face to face, but they won't be hatching elaborate plans to take over a starship...invaders from space is ancient science fiction nonsense, and you're smart enough to realize that."

"We're Columbus."

A tear welled in the corner of her eye and her lip quivered slightly. "You're not making any sense."

"We're sailing through the stars, explorers, just like Colum-bus. But to any species that actually lives out here, we *are* invaders from space. Maybe they're afraid, and this is their way of protecting—"

"We're a run-down geological survey ship from a distant mining company. What possible threat could we be to anyone?"

He glanced across the room. The group at the other table quietly plotted their next move, unconcerned. He told Carla,

"Columbus was just looking for spices when he wiped out thousands of indigenous people on Earth. His crew carried foreign diseases that the natives had no immunity to."

Carla let go of her medallion, wiped her eye, and held up her hands. "Okay, fine, if this is real, why can't I see what you see?"

He rubbed his aching shoulder. "I don't know why. We've breathed the same canned air, eaten the same crap..."

*Pressure-induced psychosis?*

No! That was *bullshit!* There had to be another reason, something that was different about him, something that—

"My arm." Sean grabbed his burnt-out prosthesis and lifted it onto the table with a loud *clang.*

The worry in Carla's watery eyes seeped into her voice. "What's wrong with your arm?"

"The motors and circuits are all fried, but the neural interface must still be functioning. Maybe it makes me immune to their camouflage, lets me see what you can't."

She still looked doubtful. "Sean..."

He reached across the table for her hand, happy she did not jump or pull away. "Carla, if there's even a *chance* it could be true, you have to come with me now. I can get you real proof, proof you can see without any kind of enhancement."

"How are you going to do that?"

He thought of the Sanderson-thing lying down in the hold, of the dark serum that flowed from its wound. "I'll get you a blood sample. You can examine it, see that I'm telling the truth, maybe discover a way to beat them."

A spark in her eyes. She looked back at the other table. "Sean, how will you get—?"

"Would you believe me then?" he interjected, trying not to sound desperate.

"Yes, of course I would." She squeezed his hand, telling him she loved and trusted him without uttering a single word.

Sean smiled, relieved. "Then let's go."

A shape dropped from the ceiling, landing with a wet splat. Sean leapt back, startled, and looked up to find an open vent. When he lowered his gaze, he saw the squid. It sat among the crumbs in Carla's tray, its seven tentacles whipping around, its single black eye focused intently upon her face.

Sean pushed the tray off the table, sent it crashing to the floor. The tiny invader tried to make another escape, but this time, his boot was faster. Its soft body ruptured with an audible *pop*, spraying rosy jelly.

Carla was standing now. She backed away, her hands across her mouth, a river of tears on her cheek. She stared at the tray, then looked up at Sean.

She saw it. She believed.

Out of the corner of his eye, Sean saw the others standing, monsters playing human. He lifted his shirt and brought out the 9mm handgun, clicking off the safety as he did so. The report was as loud as a barrage from heavy artillery. Bullets sped through the air, tore into the Lee-thing's chest and exploded from its back, giving the tables behind it an oily shower. The animal fell backward, landed on the floor with a *thud*.

The Copeland alien bent down; attended to its fallen comrade. The Fritz and Montgomery-things froze in their tracks.

"I see you," Sean told them, shifting his eyes and the barrel of the gun between targets.

"Okay, you see us." It was the Fritz-thing, its mask expressionless, unreadable. It raised its hands. "We don't have anything."

"Where did you come from?" Sean wanted to know. "What the hell do you want from us?"

Silence. Blank, glassy stares.

*"WHAT DO YOU WANT!"*

The Montgomery-thing grabbed hold of Carla and pulled her back.

There was fear in Carla's eyes. She squirmed in the thing's grasp, her silver medallion swinging like a pendulum from her neck as she tried to wrestle free, tried to run to Sean's side, but the alien was clearly too strong for her.

Sean was shaking. He held the gun in his left hand and tried to steady his aim, his eyes watering. The prosthesis felt like an anchor chained to his aching right shoulder, threatening to pull him off balance and send him to the floor. "I've got survey charges planted all over this ship. Let her go, let us walk out of here, or I'll blow it up."

More silence, except from Carla. She was still crying.

"I swear to God I'll do it," he told them. *"Now let her go!"*

"Please," the Fritz-thing pleaded, "put down the gun."

"You'd like that wouldn't you?"

"Yes, I would." It motioned to the others. "We all would."

He took his eyes off the thing for just a moment, looking at Carla, his lip quivering. "Don't you hurt her."

"You're the only one hurting anyone, Sean," the Fritz-thing told him.

He snickered mirthlessly. "You try to put one of those squids in me, do God only knows what with the rest of the crew, and you say *I'm* the one hurting people?"

Carla spoke up through her tears, "Sean...please, do what she says. Put down the gun."

"It's going to be okay, honey," he assured her, and in his mind, Sean saw how it would all unfold. He would kill these three, then hunt down the remaining aliens with Carla at his side. There would be at least another four, one for every crewmember. When they got back to the station, just the two of them, they'd tell the marshals what had happened, let *them* deal with the threat. For Sean and Carla, it would all be over. They could move on, could live in the future they had planned.

A metal tray struck Sean's left hand, sent a bolt of agony through his wrist and thumb, and caused him to drop the gun. He turned in time to see an alien form lunging at him. It was the Copeland-thing. Before he could act, it had him in a headlock.

Its strength was amazing.

Sean tried to break free, but the thing pushed him flat against the wall and put an elbow in his back, pinning him. Pain rang loudly throughout his body, and as the room grew dark, he heard Carla calling out his name.

---

"Sean, did you see that?" she asked, pointing toward some far-off rock formations.

He peered through his faceplate, trying to find something out-of-the-ordinary. The obsidian spires on the horizon had the appearance of long, bony fingers rising up from the loam. "See what?"

"I thought..." Carla shook her head in her helmet and snickered. "Nothing. Guess this place is starting to creep me out."

Sean gave his attention back to Orpheus, watched the rig climb the grated ramp into *Ambrosia*'s hold, then waited for the bay doors to seal. When he was certain everything was secure, he grabbed Carla by the arm and pulled her onto the lift.

As the platform began its rise toward the airlock, Carla reached for the red button on the control box.

He grabbed the railing to steady himself as they came to an abrupt halt. "What's wrong?"

She had her back to him, her gloved hand still at the controls. "I know I've been playing twenty questions with you all day, but I need to ask you just one more. It's a simple one, only needs a yes or no response."

"Yes," Sean told her.

"You haven't heard the question."

"You want to know if I'll follow you wherever you decide to go, or you want me to marry you." He moved across the platform, put his hand on the shoulder of her environment suit. "Either way, the answer is yes."

Carla pressed the green button to continue their ascent, then spun around to hug him. Their faceplates collided with the *clink* of champagne glasses, and they laughed at their own awkwardness, holding tightly to one another as klaxons blared and the airlock re-pressurized.

---

Sean opened his eyes and let them adjust to the flickering light. A fluorescent bulb in the overhead fixture was going out, adding to his disorientation. He lifted his head to look around.

Medlab.

He was lying on a patient bed in the Medlab.

Sean attempted to move his prosthesis, then remembered it had shorted out. When he tried to move his left arm, however, he found it paralyzed as well. He glanced down his torso and saw that he was tightly restrained.

The beds on either side of him were also occupied, bodies covered over in bloodstained plastic. Corpses.

He strained against his bonds, rocking and pulling at the straps until his shoulder cried for him to stop and lay still. He opened his mouth to call for help, but there was no one to yell out to.

The loud hiss of an opening hatch filled the chamber, followed by the *click-clack* of shoes on flooring, growing louder as they approached. "Sean? Sean, are you awake?"

Carla's voice.

He rose up as far as his restraints would allow. "Are you okay? What did they do to you?"

She stood over him, running her hand across his sweaty forehead and through his dampened hair. "I'm fine, Sean. They didn't do anything to me. I'm fine."

He relaxed. "Oh, thank God! Thank God!"

"Sean..."

"I just remembered something," he told her. "When we were out on the asteroid, you said you saw something. What did you see?"

Carla blinked, then shook her head. "Nothing. My mind was playing tricks on me, just like your mind's been playing tricks on you."

"*My* mind?" He tried to rise up again. "No. You saw the squid with your own eyes. And on the asteroid...you saw something there too. What did you see? Was it one of them?—was it—?"

"*Sean!*" Carla swallowed. She looked close to tears. "Listen to me...you've *killed* people. Doctor Edwards, Sanderson, Lee. They're dead."

He tilted his head to either side, looking at the covered bodies. The blood that streaked the translucent plastic was red. Human. He turned back to Carla, his mouth open and dry.

"I know you didn't mean to do it," she told him. "You're

sick. We got into the doctor's office. I read his notes. Pressure-induced psychosis."

"No," Sean said, over and over again, "No."

Carla continued to wipe his forehead. "I know you'd never intentionally hurt anyone. That's why I have to ask...where are the charges?"

"There aren't any aliens?" His voice was weak and childlike.

"No, Sean," she told him. "There are no aliens, no squids. You threw my tray to the floor and stomped on a packet of Smucker's. You scared the hell out of me. And then when you shot Lee..."

She put a hand to her eye and turned away.

The realization of what Carla was telling him, of what he had done, slowly sank into his brain. He'd killed his friends...his family. Desolate tears flowed, blurring his vision. "Oh...*God!*"

"Shhhh." She took the sleeve of her flight jacket and dried his eyes. "I can help you, cure you, make it so you won't see these things anymore, but first I need you to...to tell me where you put the explosives."

"*I'm so sorry,*" he cried.

"I know, baby." She sniffled and swallowed, her eyes glistening in the strobing light. "The medicine...it's going to...you're going to sleep for a while, so we really need to know where you hid those charges now, need to make sure we can deactivate them before they go off. I know you don't want anybody else to get hurt."

"I love you," he told her, fighting back new tears.

An odd look came over Carla's face, as if she were searching for the right response, and Sean wondered if the things he'd done were so horrible that all she could feel toward him now was disgust.

"Look, I love you too..." Her watery eyes skirted his as she spoke the words. She blinked a single drop out onto her cheek and it ran the length of her face to dangle from her chin.

Sean gave an understanding nod, fresh tears scorching his own cheeks as he retraced his steps for her. He told her where he placed each and every charge, pausing several times to apologize for what he had done, knowing that no apology, no matter how sincere, would ever be enough to repair the damage.

When she had all the locations, Carla leaned in to kiss him on the forehead "Now I can give you what you need to get well."

Sean felt a sting, and as the needle slid inside his vein, he noticed something strange.

He didn't see a Saint Albert's medallion around her neck.

# FOR HER

Brooke wanted to have a threesome.

Not that Jeff was complaining. Sex with two women at once was the fantasy of every straight, red-blooded American man. But as this Nevada highway unfurled beneath the glare of his headlights, and the time and place for the actual event drew nearer with each passing mile, a nervous dread nestled in the pit of his stomach, feeding him the same question again and again:

*Does she want to leave me for someone else?*

Brooke's appetite for sex was ravenous, insatiable, and despite five years of marriage, the ghosts of imagined infidelities still haunted the darkness at the back of Jeff's mind. He pictured her having affairs with men who were more muscular, or younger, or just plain *bigger* than he was, but in all of his insecure, paranoid delusions, he'd never once thought of her in bed with another woman.

Such a scenario suddenly played out behind his eyes, and he had to fight to maintain control of the Durango's wheel, his tires kicking up sand as they momentarily left the asphalt.

"Careful there, Tiger." Brooke's hand pressed the Mapquest directions flat against her muscular thigh. "I'd like to get there in one piece. Are you falling asleep?"

"Not on your life," he told her, managing a smile.

She grinned back and ran her fingers through her blonde mane, exposing the multitude of golden hoops that pierced her ear. The Japanese character for "love" was tattooed on the side of her neck, just above her left shoulder. Jeff glanced down at Brooke's hip, finding the latest addition to her body art collection peeking out from beneath the waistband of her shorts. A bright blue serpent with mottled, feathery wings etched onto its scaly back. She had it done the day she asked him to take her to this whorehouse.

At first, Jeff had been apprehensive. The idea of sex with a prostitute provoked nightmare visions where his cock turned black and rotted off. But Brooke wouldn't let it go, and she'd done her homework. The ladies, she'd told him, were tested prior to reporting for duty; they worked seven days straight, and could not leave the property for any reason during that shift; and since condom use was mandated by state law, there had been no cases—zero—where the customer of a legal brothel contracted a deadly disease. Finally, his wife showed him the profile of the working girl she had in mind—a curvy Latin lovely with the exotic name of Xilomen—and there was no way he could say no.

But Jeff couldn't stop wondering why she wanted it so badly.

He told himself it was just another kink she needed to get out of her system, and he was happy she hadn't gone behind his back to do it, happy she wanted him there to experience it with her.

Still, as Jeff chauffeured his wife toward this rendezvous with a woman they'd never met, he couldn't help but wonder if she secretly preferred women. He'd seen enough talk shows to know such things happened to people who'd been married much longer. Out of the blue, their spouses sat them down and told them they were gay. Either they had recently discovered feelings for someone of the same sex, or worse, they'd been fighting those longings their entire life, marrying only to conform to societal norms. It was a crazy idea, but he couldn't shake it, and it led him back to that same worrisome question:

*Does she want to leave me for someone else?*

Brooke read aloud from her directions, the stud that skewered her tongue glinting like a diamond as she spoke, "Turn left onto Cottontail Drive. Point one miles. End at the Bunny Hop Ranch."

He peered into the darkness at the edge of his headlights. "I don't suppose we'd be lucky enough to get a sign."

As if on cue, a flashing red speck illuminated the gloom ahead, growing larger and brighter as they approached until it became a blazing neon arrow, pointing them toward a dirt road. Beneath this arrow, a wooden billboard featured an airbrushed female rabbit in black lingerie. With its long eyelashes and glossy red lips, the drawing reminded Jeff of those old Warner Brothers cartoons where Bugs Bunny dressed in drag, but this particular bunny had size double-D breasts. The cartoon sat atop a Bunny Hop Ranch logo, kicking up its black stiletto heels. Off to the side, a tagline read: "Heaven is just a jump away."

Brooke giggled. "How's that for a sign?"

A turn of the wheel took them onto the side road, the glow of the neon arrow transforming the sands into a Martian landscape.

"They've made the whole desert a red-light district," Jeff said with a laugh, keeping his eyes forward. It was hard to tell where the road stopped and the desert began.

"I think they use red because it's the color of the heart." Her voice was breathy, the way she talked when she was touching herself, trying to get him in the mood. "Red is the color of *passion*."

He was about to look over at her, to see if she had her hands in her shorts, but then he saw the house.

Roman columns lined a long, plantation-style porch. Wings branched off from either side of the main house like open arms, each covered in windows, making it appear as if there were a hundred rooms within. White-painted walls were bathed in the glow of spotlights, granting it the appearance of a country inn or house of worship, not a den of sin.

"Wow," he said. "Check this place out."

Brooke reached across the seat for his hand. "Do I have good taste, or what?"

Jeff gave her fingers a light squeeze, his heart beating quicker within his chest. This was it. They were actually going to do this.

Half a dozen cars and trucks sat parked in the sand beside the house. He steered the Durango over to join them, then turned to his wife, taking in her beauty.

"You ready?" he asked.

"Oh yeah." She leaned forward, kissing him softly. "*You're* going to enjoy it, aren't you?"

"I enjoy anything that makes you happy, Brooke," he told her.

"I want to make you happy too." She smiled lovingly, kissing him again even as her hand went to the door.

They started toward the entrance, walking hand-in-hand. Jeff's eyes ran from window to window. Some were dark, others lit, but all had thick, drawn drapes that barred any glimpse of the interior.

"You know," Brooke said, "when I was in college, I thought about working in a brothel."

He tried to sound shocked, "Really?"

"Sure," she confirmed. "I mean, here I was, the only state where it's actually legal to have sex all day long and get paid for it. Talk about your dream job."

The joy in her voice made his stomach sink. "Why didn't you?"

"I fell in love," she told him, then laid her head on his shoulder as they walked. "And I knew I wanted to be with you forever."

Jeff wished he could believe her.

———

A beautiful Asian girl sat behind a desk in the foyer, her nose in a book titled *Chocolate Park*. Jeff had a thing for Asian girls. His eyes traveled over her flaxen skin and down the inky tresses that pooled on her shoulders. For a moment, he considered asking her if *she* was available for their party, but he quickly thought better of it. She could've been hired solely to answer phones and greet guests, and insinuating that she was a whore might just get him smacked. Besides, Brooke had her heart set on this Xilomen.

*You're here for her, remember, not you. For her.*

"Excuse me," he said.

The Asian girl stopped reading and smiled. "Welcome to The Ranch. I'm Tanya. How can I help you?"

"We booked a 'couple's party.'"

"Very nice." Tanya set her book aside, turning her attention to a large day planner that lay open on the desk. "Name?"

"Kendall."

"You booked Xilomen." A knowing grin bloomed on her

lips. She picked up a phone; put it to her ear. "I'll call her down for you."

On the wall behind the desk hung a large sign with the heading "Sexual Menu." Below the title, various sex acts and services were described in great detail, as if each was a meal to be savored in some fancy restaurant. And just like a fine bill of fare, there were no prices.

"Do you know how much this party will cost?" Jeff asked.

Tanya put her hand over the receiver. "Sorry. All the girls are independent contractors. You'll have to negotiate that with —" She uncovered the phone, said, "The Kendalls are here for you," then hung up and looked at him. "She'll be right down. Is this your first time to party with us?"

He snickered. "That obvious, huh?"

"Don't worry," the receptionist assured them as she sat back and reached for her book. "Xilo's the best. She'll take good care of you."

"Now you've done it, Tanya," a voice called out, turning Jeff's head.

A tall, bronze-skinned woman descended a spiral staircase, joining them on floor of the tiled lobby. Dark brown locks cascaded over her shoulders and down her back, ending at the slender waist of a tight, black dress that showcased her figure. It was a body that promised a night he would never forget.

"You've built up their expectations," she said with a hint of accent. "Now they can't help but be disappointed with me."

Brooke looked at Jeff and laughed. "Judging by the way my husband's mouth is hanging open, I don't think you have anything to worry about."

He noticed an odd tone to his wife's voice, almost like jealousy, but her grin said otherwise.

Their date's smile widened, her dazzling teeth sparkling like pearls between the rose petals of her lips. She slinked over, her long, slender legs ending in black stilettos. "I'm Xilomen, but please, call me Xilo—like J-Lo, but with a Z."

When she slipped her arm in his and escorted them down a hall, Jeff heard chains rattle and slap against wood. His eyes rose to the ceiling. "What was that?"

"One of the girls is entertaining upstairs," Xilo told them matter-of-factly. "Some of our clients enjoy a little bondage."

"Jeff likes it when I tie *him* up," Brooke announced.

"Reeeally?" Xilo flashed a demure grin. "Well, we'll have to see what we can do about that."

He glanced back at his wife, shocked that she would share such an intimate detail, but then he thought, *Relax, you're both gonna fuck this girl in a minute.*

Xilomen opened a door to her left and motioned for them to enter.

According to their website, the ranch had various party suites, each decorated according to its own theme. Jeff had liked the marble columns and statuary of Roman Holiday, but Brooke wanted to party in Paradise Cove.

"It reminds me of our honeymoon in Cancun," she'd told him.

This room, however, was no larger than a walk-in closet. Red drapes hung from floor to ceiling on all four walls, and a tiny security camera was mounted near the ceiling in the corner. Xilo closed the door behind them and stood with her back to the lens.

"I hate talking money," she said. "I much prefer pleasure, which is why we get all that pesky business stuff out of the way up front, so we can move on to..." Her gaze lowered to the crotch of Jeff's jeans. "...bigger and better things."

Brooke smiled at her husband. "And believe me, you won't be disappointed there."

Jeff chuckled; glad to hear Brooke was happy with his

manhood. *See, you satisfy her. She's not going to leave you for this woman or anybody else. Stop your worrying and just enjoy yourself. This is The Fantasy, man!*

"So..." Xilo's eyes rose to meet his. "How much were you thinking of spending with me tonight?"

He shrugged. "I don't know...the suite, and...everything else. Will five hundred cover it?"

Xilo giggled, then held up her hand and cleared her throat. "I'm sorry, I didn't mean to laugh, I know this is your first time." She pointed to the video camera behind her. "See, that's 'The House.' They're watching to see how much our little party is going to make for them. They get half of everything we earn here. So, if I took five hundred from you, I'd only really earn two-fifty."

Jeff looked into the lens, his stomach fluttering. "You need a thousand?"

She smiled sweetly. "If you triple that, I think we can have a real nice party."

"*Three* thousand?" Maybe he'd seen too many movies or *Law & Order* episodes, where the hookers charged guys twenty bucks for a blow job, but he wasn't expecting anything close to that amount. "Is that for the whole night?"

"It would be for a few hours. To have me overnight, wow, that would be close to five figures."

Jeff's eyes widened and shot to Brooke.

"Relax," his wife told him, reaching into her purse. "You take Visa and Mastercard, don't you?"

Xilo nodded. "American Express too."

Jeff grabbed Brooke's arm. "Hon, you can't be serious."

"Don't worry." She gave his hand a gentle squeeze. "My card, my treat."

Paradise Cove featured faux-bamboo walls, an imitation palm-thatched ceiling, and painted windows that opened onto a painted sea. In the corner, silk ferns and palms surrounded a huge, kidney-shaped tub, forming a secluded rainforest grotto.

Jeff took off his watch and shoes. "So how long have you worked here?"

Xilomen chuckled as she drew a bath. "You mean how long have I been a whore?"

His face warmed. "Okay, yeah."

"A long time." She kicked off her heels and sat on the edge of the tub, moving her hand through the water to check the temperature, her reflection riding the ripples.

"Well, how long have you been in the U.S.?"

"I've been here for many years. The people who took control of my country..." Her face clouded over for a moment. "There was torture, persecution, but my mother saved me and brought me here for a better life."

Jeff nodded, wondering if selling her body night after night was the "better life" Xilo's mother had envisioned. He took off his shirt and tossed it onto a wicker chair in the corner, sweat beading on his chest, back, and forehead. It could've been nerves, but he thought it was more likely the Viagra. Xilo had offered it to him, and he'd taken it gladly, wanting to make certain they got their money's worth.

Brooke unbuttoned her blouse. The butterfly etched on her left breast looked as if it were trying to escape the jaws of the winged serpent at her hip.

Xilo saw the markings and smiled. "*Cihuacoatl.*"

Jeff didn't speak Spanish. "Excuse me?"

His wife snickered and her hands went to her panty line, stretching her skin to flatten the artwork. "She's talking about my tattoo. It's *Cihuacoatl*, the Aztec serpent goddess, 'mother of humanity.'"

"That's right." Xilo sounded impressed. "But She didn't create us all at once. Women were formed first. Men came much later, made from *tonalli*, the blood of the womb."

Jeff gave his wife's new body art more scrutiny. She'd never told him the meaning behind it, only that she thought it was cool.

Xilo shut off the faucet, then moved toward Brooke. Minus their heels, they were the same height, no taller than Jeff's chin. "You know, during certain rituals, the women who worshiped *Cihuacoatl* would explore each other... sexually."

She leaned in, hesitated; when she saw that Brooke did not shy away, she kissed her. It began as a gentle peck, then grew in intensity, their tongues probing each other's mouths with great enthusiasm.

As Jeff sat there, hypnotized by desire, his jeans grew tight. He tugged at the zipper and quickly shed them, liberating his erection.

"Why haven't I heard about this religion?" Brooke asked, a string of saliva still tethering her lips to Xilo's. "I would've signed up years ago."

"Spanish Conquistadors found homosexuality evil." Xilo reached up and undid the clasps of Brooke's bra, sliding the straps off her shoulders and down her arms. "They took the followers of *Cihuacoatl*, staked them to the ground, and set them on fire. Later, Jesuits destroyed the Aztec libraries, trying to eradicate any hint that they ever existed. Even today, the government of Peru destroys any pottery it unearths with same-sex images. They say it 'insults their national honor.'"

Xilo lowered her head to Brooke's perky, rose-tipped breast, tracing the butterfly marking with her tongue.

"You never see a woman with a caterpillar tattoo," she said between licks. "Caterpillars are ugly. They do nothing but eat, sleep, and fight with one another. But then the creator steps in, as if to correct a mistake, and they are transformed, they turn into something truly wonderful, and then all women want them."

Jeff saw Brooke shut her eyes, chewing her lower lip as Xilo's mouth closed around the firm nub of her nipple. It was the same face she made when *he* worked on her breasts, and now, to see her get identical satisfaction from the touch of a woman filled him with an odd brew of envy and excitement.

When Brooke opened her eyes again, she looked at him and smiled. "I think my husband needs some attention."

Xilomen stood and took Brooke by the hand, offering Jeff a lascivious grin. "I know just the thing."

They walked over to the bedside table. Xilo opened the drawer and took out a handful of scarves. "You take his hands; I'll do his feet."

Brooke giggled. She took hold of Jeff's wrist and wrapped it in sheer fabric.

He frowned and pulled away. "I don't know if I feel comfortable—"

"Pleeeease," his wife begged. "Do it for me."

*Give her what she wants, buddy. You don't want her to leave you.*

He reluctantly offered up his hand again.

"Now lay down," Brooke instructed.

Jeff did as he was told, allowing the women to lash his limbs to the bed frame. Xilo hummed as she tightened the knots, and he lifted his head to look at her. "What's that?"

"Oh, we were talking about *Cihuacoatl*, and I remembered a hymn my mother taught me." She cleared her throat, then sang, "*She comes forth, plumed with feathers, painted with blood, She is our mother, a goddess of war, our mother a goddess of war...*"

"You've got a great voice," Brooke told her, finishing the last of the knots.

Xilo smiled, then reached up and slid the spaghetti straps from her shoulders, allowing her black dress to fall to the floor. Her naked body surpassed even Jeff's wildest expectations. She motioned for Brooke to join her at the foot of the bed, and the two women knelt on either side of him, exchanging a playful glance across his erection before bringing it to their soft, full lips.

Jeff relaxed, let his arms and legs hang, let his head fall back against the satin pillow, and concentrated on the feel of warm, wet mouths; the gorgeous friction of their fingers as they massaged his length. Even with his eyes pinched shut he could tell who was who. The metal stud of Brooke's piercing raked and tickled his most sensitive flesh; the tip of Xilo's tongue slithered its way up his shaft in a serpentine motion.

And then they stopped.

He opened his eyes and looked down the length of the bed as Xilomen climbed onto him. She positioned herself over his erection, then sank onto his lap. As he slid deep into the moist shadows between her legs, Jeff groaned with pleasure, then realized he wasn't wearing a condom.

Before he could say anything, Brooke straddled his face. She grabbed the headboard and pressed herself against his open mouth until her pubic bone flattened his nose. Thick fluid bathed his tongue in a sudden glut. It was warm, salty.

*Blood!*

It ran down the back of Jeff's throat, gagging him.

He squirmed, and kicked; his bonds snapped taught and strangled his wrists and ankles, but his wife seemed not to notice. She seized him by the hair and held him down with her weight.

*Does she know I can't breath?* his shocked brain wondered. *I'm drowning, drowning in blood!*

Suddenly, as if she'd heard his thoughts, Brooke released

her grip and rolled off this face, scarlet tears staining her milky inner thighs.

She was smiling.

Jeff coughed up rosy spittle. It rained into his eyes and ran from the corners of his mouth as he tried to draw breath. "What the...*blood!*"

"*Tonalli,*" Xilo corrected, mounting him as if nothing had happened. She placed her palms on his chest and leaned in, her body moving up and down, her eyes locking with his as she spoke. "It is the 'animating spirit.' Without it, everything stops. There can be no joy without blood. No love. No future. No *life.*"

Brooke gave Xilo a long, passionate kiss, then knelt beside the bed, her fingers combing Jeff's sweaty hair. "It's okay, baby," she told him. "She'll be here soon. It's going to be wonderful, you'll see."

Jeff stared at his wife, uncomprehending. He pulled on his restraints to no avail, then turned his attention to the woman on his lap. "Get off me, you sick bitch! Let me up!"

"When we're finished," Xilomen assured him, moving her hips, making his penetrations deeper and even more silken.

"*Now!*"

Xilo ignored him. She closed her eyes and continued to ride him as she sang the rest of *Cihuacoatl's* hymn, "*She comes forth, She appears when war is waged, She protects us in war, that we shall not be destroyed, that we shall never be parted...*"

The door creaked open and someone entered the room. Jeff strained his neck to see who it was and caught a glimpse of rainbow feathers, just like Brooke's tattoo.

*It can't be...*

He glared at his wife, her menstrual blood cooling on his lips as he screamed, "*Untie me!*"

She ran her fingers through his hair, but said nothing.

He heard a long hiss, like a slashed tire breathing its last. His heart hammered and he frantically pulled at his bonds, rattling the bedframe. *"Brooke!"*

"We're saving you," she told him, her voice calm and loving, her eyes aglow. "Now I'll never lose you. We'll be together forever."

The blue pill continued to work its magic, keeping Jeff's cock an iron rod in spite of his fear, and Xilomen impaled herself upon it again and again, chanting, *"She comes adorned in the ancient manner, plumed with feathers...plumed with...feathers..."*

Brooke looked up and smiled with excitement. "She's here."

Jeff turned his head, following his wife's line of sight, and his gaze was met by reptilian eyes the size of footballs. Bright peacock quills crowned the serpent's forehead, and long, slender arms hung from its sides. Its thin, scaly lips peeled back, revealing fangs like walrus tusks. His body tensed, expecting the animal to strike. Instead, it kept its distance, its massive head swaying back and forth, holding Jeff in its gaze as if Brooke and Xilo were not even in the room.

A rattlesnake's jangle filled the air, providing music for Xilo's lyrics.

*"She comes forth,"* she crooned, breathing harder, her hips moving faster, *"our mother, a goddess..."*

Jeff's mouth was dry, mute. He closed his eyes, hoping that this was just a nightmare, that his fear of losing his wife had finally pulled him over the edge, dragging him down into an abyss of madness.

*"She comes forth, She comes...She comes..."* Xilomen cried out in ecstasy, and Jeff's eyes sprang open to stare into the gutted sockets of a charred skull. The young beauty from the Internet was gone, replaced by a seared corpse that was somehow able to move. Her scorched hand reached down, her brittle fingers

caressing his cheek. The blackened, leathery skin around her teeth pulled back to form a grotesque grin, and she finished her song, "...*to make you an example and a companion.*"

Jeff tried to scream, but all he could manage was a dry, cracked whine. He tilted his head toward Brooke, but his wife didn't seem the least bit shocked. Either she couldn't see the ghoul that mounted him, or she'd seen it before.

*Cihuacoatl* rattled and hissed, and the cacophony became deafening. It reached out, its claw touching his chest, the hot fingers sinking into his flesh as if it were butter. He felt his bones crack and expand, felt the skin come loose from its moorings and drift across his body, congealing into odd, alien formations, and then the room was bathed in blinding blue light.

---

Brooke climbed the stairs. Her last client had been overweight, hairy, more ape than human being, and he came far too quickly. At least his money had been good.

Now what she needed was a *real* man.

Before bringing Jeff here to the ranch, she'd been afraid he would leave her. She wasn't blind. She noticed the way he looked at other women, especially Asian women, and in her mind, she saw him having affairs with girls who were taller, younger, thinner, or just more exotic-looking than she was. And when they arrived here that first night, when her husband saw Tanya, the receptionist, and undressed her with his eyes, she knew she'd made the right decision.

Brooke had originally looked at a threesome as a way for Jeff to get those fantasies out of his system, a way to share the experience and keep him from going behind her back. The quest for to make him happy led her here, to a secret meeting with Xilomen, where she learned the truth of *Cihuacoatl's* power and was shown the promise of eternal life, of youth and beauty long after death. Now they would always be together, and she would have her husband's love for all time.

*Thank the goddess for saving our marriage, for saving us!*

She opened the door to her room, but left the light off. "Jeff?"

His eyes shone like twin lamps, illuminating the darkened corner. Buds of sinew flapped and waved along his sides, and the chain that hung from his collar jingled and slapped the wooden floor.

He was excited to see her.

Jeff used his lengthy new appendages to crawl up onto the bed. A long, glistening tongue hung from his mandibles, and a massive erection reached out from his pelvis like a fisted arm.

Brooke licked her lips as she closed the door.

It was all for her.

# SANCTUARY

Snow, merciless, all consuming, carried on the backs of the howling winds; it choked the mountain pass, filling in footprints, blocking out the brightness of the moon, a moon that had seemed so large in the sky, so close, closer here than at any other point on Earth. Zhang Lau trudged on; his Soviet-made RPD machine gun slung over his shoulder, slapping his back with every step, his dark eyebrows now white with ice. He trudged on because to remain still was certain death; death from the biting cold, from the deepening snow, from the dark thing that moved rapidly through it all, stalking ever nearer, the thing that had torn four of his men apart.

Li Tung was at his side, stumbling through the mounting drifts, rapidly carving deep furrows that were just as quickly erased. "What——?"

The rest was lost beneath the whistling wind.

"Keep moving!" Zhang shouted; a natural commander now validated by rank. He dared a backward glance, saw nothing, but knew it was there just the same. He drew the collar of his standard-issue coat closed with gloved hands, covering chapped lips. Frozen as he was, he found he was sweating beneath his fur-lined cap.

An hour ago, they'd been riding horses. Now, those animals lay in pieces, buried in an icy tomb with what remained of his unit, his friends.

*An army of the people is invincible*, the posters all proclaimed.

Zhang now wished that had been more than party propaganda.

He climbed higher, every breath a fog that blurred his path, every movement a struggle; the swelling white tide enveloped him in its frigid embrace, urging him to slow down, to rest, but fear was a forceful hand upon his back, pushing him onward, upward, blinding him with flashes of nightmare imagery; snow like fresh rice paper, soaking up red ink-a demon scrawling horrid calligraphy with its claws and fangs. He remembered eyes; they burned through the storm like-

*Torches!*

Flames danced on the wind, burning oil, illuminating steps built into the mountainside as if hewn from the Himalayan rock.

A howl rose above the whistling storm, unearthly, predatory. It echoed through the pass, disorientating, betraying nothing of the owner's true location.

Zhang tugged on Li's shoulder, pulling him wordlessly toward the stairs. They climbed quickly, and the first yowl was answered by a second, then a third, joining together to form a chilling chorus. When a fourth cry reached their frozen ears, the men were already halfway up the steps.

The whirling snow teased Zhang's eyes, allowing him only faint glimpses of the structure waiting for them at the summit; a Chinese-style roof silhouetted against a pale night sky. Deer antlers sprouted from its eaves, making the building appear to have horns.

Someone had to be inside, had to let them in.

Zhang reached the final step and threw himself against the entrance; pounded the wood with numb fists, screamed vapor into the wind. He pressed his ear against the snow-covered wood; heard the slide of a bolt. The huge doors swung inward at last and a bald monk stood there smiling.

"*Tashi delek*," the monk said with a slight bow. "We were not expecting to have——"

Zhang pushed past him, dragged Li inside. "Close the doors!"

The monk's smile never wavered. He glanced out into the storm; his saffron robes billowed like sails in a typhoon. "Are there no more——?"

"*Close them!*" Zhang tried to stand tall; to look imposing, threatening, but his arms and legs were shaking uncontrollably.

The monk studied them for what seemed like an eternity. His bright eyes alternated between the machine guns slung across their backs and the single red stars stitched onto their caps. Finally, he turned away and pushed the thick, heavy doors closed against the wind, cutting its whistle off sharply. He then secured the opening with a huge bolt forged of solid iron.

Zhang hoped it would be enough to keep the howling things at bay.

He frowned, still trembling despite the newfound warmth of this monastery. Countless candles burned; the numbing frost melted, soaking his uniform, dripping slowly, rhythmically onto his boots and the stone flooring beneath. Columns lined the center of the vast chamber, creating a carpeted hallway to the statue at the far end-a golden Buddha, sitting cross-legged, its sculpted face smiling as the monk at the door had been smiling. Other monks lined either side of the hall; dozens of them, all mimicked the statue, all chanted endlessly. None looked up at Zhang, or at Li; none showed any interest at all.

The monk at the door took a step forward, motioned toward the cavernous hall. "Come, let me get you men some tea to warm your bones."

Zhang was slow to take his eyes from the door, half expecting a shower of splinters as clawed hands punched their way through to get inside, to get *him*. His lips quivered; his teeth chattered. "Th-th-" He forced it out, "*Thank* you."

As the monk rushed past them, Li turned his head toward Zhang in a jerky, birdlike motion and managed a single world, "Safe?"

Zhang gave a hesitant nod and followed their new host into the great hall, casting quick glances over his shoulder at the door as they moved away.

The monastery stank. Spicy incense and pungent oils burned, joining forces to combat the musty smells lurking just below-the reek of yak hair and rugs, soaked by melting snow and ice, by human sweat, and left to dry in this stale air; the unpleasant perfume of a place long closed off from the outside world.

"I am Yeshe," the monk said without looking back at them, then he held out his hands, indicating his many brothers who sat chanting on either side. "We live a simple life, but what little we have is yours."

*What* little *you have?*

Zhang's gaze journeyed around the vast chamber; lingered a moment on a pair of sculpted dragons that clung to the rafters-solid gold, their jeweled eyes sparkling in the firelight, then moved on to the prayer bells that hung from every column-also gold, and finally landed on the enormous golden Buddha at the far end of the hall. So much wealth, tucked away here at the top of the world, buried in ice, when his home village and others like it lived in poverty and starvation. The sale of but one of these items could feed his entire family for a lifetime.

Something moved in the tail of Zhang's eye; a dark, skulking shape. He spun toward it, his still-frozen hands moving instinctively to the comfort of his machine gun, his head a blur of claws, of teeth, of strong, able-bodied men reduced to steaming entrails, and he saw-

A young woman.

She'd pulled an embroidered door curtain aside to peek in on them. Her long, black hair nearly swept the floor.

"Dohna," the monk, Yeshe, called out.

The girl stepped into the light, her head bowed. She wore a white *chuba*, a robe made from sheepskin; the black belt around her thin waist kept it closed. "Yes, *Trapa-la?*"

"Our friends have traveled far in bitter cold," Yeshe informed her. "Bring *cha süma.*"

Her dark eyes lifted, regarded Zhang through raven strands, and then she was gone, the door tapestry swaying leisurely in her wake.

Zhang turned back to Yeshe. "She called you *Trapa-la?*"

"A term of respect," he told them. "I am abbot to this monastery. You're Chinese, yes?"

Zhang nodded absently, his mind still on the girl. "Henan province."

"You're a long way from home. Tell me, what brings you to the roof of the world?"

"Your leaders signed an agreement with the Chinese government. We're here to liberate you, protect you."

Yeshe shook his bald head slowly. "I know nothing of this 'agreement.'" He led them to the foot of the massive Buddha; large pillows placed evenly on rugs, and motioned for them to take a seat. "But I can assure you that we are in no need of your protection here."

"Of course not." Li knelt, fell back onto his pillow, and rippled with muted laughter until tears welled in his eyes. "What protection can there be from monsters?"

"Monsters?" Yeshe looked from Li to Zhang inquisitively as he took his place next to them on the rugs.

"I don't think we can hope to convince you of what we've seen," Zhang explained. "I'm not sure that even I'm convinced of it, and I was there."

The girl, Dohna, reappeared. A metal tray formed a shelf across her outstretched arms, and on it, an ornate copper teapot with three wooden bowls—two small and one large. She made her way quickly yet carefully over to where the three men sat, then knelt down before them. When the tray was flat on the rug, she took the copper pot and gently tipped it, pouring liquid into the bowls and passing them out. Yeshe received the largest of the bowls, Zhang and Li the smaller two.

Zhang felt warmth soak through the wood into his hands and was grateful for it. The concoction inside, however, did not look like any tea he'd ever seen before in his life. It was like thick oil; crowned with scummy yellow foam.

"*Cha süma*," Yeshe announced with that pleasant smile of his. "Butter tea. Dohna churns it for us."

Zhang lifted his eyes to the girl. She sat frozen; head bowed, one hand in her lap, the other on the teapot's copper handle. Her long hair draped over her shoulders and ample breasts like a black shawl.

"Thank you," he told her.

Dohna offered only a slight nod in reply.

Zhang took a long sip, letting the hot drink bathe his

tongue. He winced at the taste and quickly swallowed, the warmth filling him, chasing off any lingering chill.

Li was more hesitant, but he too drank of the tea.

Dohna lifted the copper teapot and moved toward them once more. Half her face lay hidden behind the curtain of her hair. Her single visible eye focused on her work, she filled each of their bowls back to the brim.

Yeshe noticed their surprise. "It is custom," he informed them. "After every sip, the guest's bowl is topped off. In this way, their bowl, their *good luck*, is never drained."

Zhang nodded, but his eyes never left Dohna. He reached for her, ran his fingers through her shining tresses. *Like strands of fine silk.* "I thought nuns shaved their heads?"

Dohna jerked away from him. "I'm *not* a nun."

Her voice was soft, her tone injured.

Zhang held up his hand. "I meant no insult."

"I was taken from my family years ago," she told him, "brought here to serve the gurus, to protect dharma."

Zhang offered her an understanding nod, thinking of his own conscription, how his own mother had cried as he was led from his village, his *home*, never to return.

Yeshe spoke up. "Dohna and others like her serve our earthly needs, so that we may concern ourselves with purely spiritual matters."

"I see." Zhang wanted to smile, but looking at Dohna -her dark, sad eyes; pale skin that had rarely been kissed by the sun; her full, expressionless lips-it was impossible to muster even a polite grin.

"You spoke of monsters?" Yeshe said, changing the subject.

"Yes," Zhang replied. "Monsters."

*Monsters who take children from the love of their families and exile them to the cold, to the-*

"—Nightmares. They came with the storm; fell on us when we entered this mountain pass. It happened so quickly... I..." He swallowed hard, trying to keep the bloody images away from his eyes, to force them back down into the dark. "I've heard the stories...tales of creatures roaming these mountains, big-footed apes who walk like men."

"Yeti?" Yeshe laughed briefly, humorlessly, then his eyes and voice turned serious. "No, friends...you saw no yeti here."

"*Something* killed my men," Zhang assured him. "If not the yeti, then-" He stopped. Wild, hungry howls seeped through the monastery walls. Beside him, Li stiffened, and together, their wide eyes shot toward the door at the opposite end of the hall.

The monks on the floor gave no sign of acknowledgement. They continued to chant; eyes forward, arms and legs crossed, heads nodding slightly, the stream of words that flowed from their mouths an endless, meaningless drone.

"What are they?" Zhang finished.

"*Mamo*," Dohna told them.

Zhang and Li gave her their full attention.

Her dark eyes were on the bolted door, but she showed no fear. "Powerful *dakini*." She tilted her head toward Zhang. "Demons."

"Demons," Zhang repeated.

She nodded. "Cunning, ferocious...it is said they once attacked the lord Buddha himself, as he meditated in the shade of the tree of enlightenment." At that, her gaze rose to the downcast face of the golden Buddha, and her expressionless lips curled into a beautiful, awe-struck grin.

Another long, baleful howl. Louder. Nearer.

Li instantly scurried backward on all fours; huddled up against the base of the statue, his hands clamped over his ears.

"Keep it away!" he cried. "I won't die like the others. Not like that."

"No one else is going to die," Zhang promised. He turned back to Yeshe, pleading, "What can we do?"

The monk sat calmly on his pillow, seemingly unconcerned. "Of all the gods and demons, *mamo* are the most vicious." He nodded at the machine gun strapped to Zhang's back. "Bullets cannot stop them, but they can be subdued."

"How?" Zhang wanted to know.

Yeshe motioned toward the other monks that filled the hall. "Our chant pacifies the turmoil of the *mamo*. So long as the chant continues, we have nothing to fear from them."

Li had stripped off his backpack. It sat on the rug in front of him, forming an island between him and the door. He had his machine gun, but his finger wasn't on the trigger. Instead, he held it in both hands as if it was a bow staff; ready to spar with whoever or whatever came near him in the night.

Yeshe took another long sip from his bowl, then said, "You are both welcomed to stay and wait for fairer weather. The *mamo* came with the storm, perhaps they will leave with it as well."

Dohna refilled the monk's bowl with rancid tea, her sad eyes drifting over to Zhang, awaiting his answer.

Zhang's gaze locked with hers a moment, drinking in her beauty, then shifted back to Yeshe. "Thank you, *Trapa-la*. You are most kind."

Another long howl made Li shriek.

———

"I'll take care of you," Zhang told him. "I won't let anything bad happen."

They were outside once more, far from the dank warmth

of the monastery, still a long way from home. The moon filled the horizon—a huge, unsympathetic eye, watching idly as they plowed through endless drifts on horseback. And while the storm had subsided, the chill remained, as did the knowledge that they were being stalked, hunted.

"We have to go back," Li called out, his voice as thin and shrill as the whistling winds. "We have to—"

A surging chorus of howls reverberated off the walls of the canyon, shaking fresh powder from the rocks overhead, giving birth to a new blizzard.

Zhang's horse reared and threw back its head, neying fog. He fought to hold onto the animal's reins; teeth clinched, breath whistling out through his nose. His eyes were no more than slits as he struggled to see what was happening around him, and his ears rang with a frightening melee of sound.

Li screamed and thunder exploded from his machine gun. The howls ended abruptly, replaced by a wave of low, hungry snarls, by the scratch and crunch of taloned feet scurrying across icy drifts, growing louder, closer. They seemed to be coming from everywhere.

Zhang saw black stains seep through the pale curtain of snowfall, feminine shadows. Their dark, emaciated breasts swung limply as they launched themselves at Li; fangs bared, eyes blazing with savage intent. Ruthless claws ripped Li's gun from his hands and the nightmare harem dragged him from his horse; shredded both his coat and the tender flesh beneath, creating a fine mist of blood that hung in the air with the waning echo of his final scream.

Li's fallen mare dug in the snow with its front hooves; eyes wide with panic, ears pinned back to block out the rending sounds of the feeding *mamo*. The horse was still trying to stand as countless fangs and talons tore it open. Panicked whinnies rose to ear-splitting shrieks, then fell off to nothing as the mare was pulled apart.

Zhang had spent half his life in combat. He'd seen the great ugliness Man was capable of, but until that moment, he had never known true barbarity.

One of the she-demons looked up from its kill; its malignant stare locked with Zhang's. Inky hair spilled from its head in wild, unkempt tangles, and its lips curled back like burning parchment; a smile full of bloodied daggers. "This shrine is not your sanctuary," the rancid thing told him, each word a tiger's growl. "It's a prison."

And then Zhang felt a hand grasp his arm. He reached out blindly, grabbed the stranger by the wrist. It was not the sharpened talon of a *mamo*. No. This hand was pale, delicate.

A human voice, female; soft as a whisper, yet able to drown out all other sound, "Forgive me. You squirmed in your sleep. It looked as if you were in pain."

*Dohna?*

Zhang sat up, and the servant girl was there, kneeling beside him on the floor of the dimly lit monastery. "A dream," he said hoarsely, the realization flooding him with sudden, inexpressible relief. Zhang glanced into the far corner; found Li sleeping with his back against the wall, machine gun still clutched in his gloved hands. "Only a dream."

"*No*, it was more than that." Dohna squeezed his arm; a child in need of protection, her fair skin painted in the warm flicker of torchlight, her voice filled with deadly urgency. "I have the visions too. Whenever I close my eyes, I see the *mamo*...out there-" Her dark eyes moved to the sealed door on the opposite end of the chamber. "-waiting for me to step outside this temple, waiting to..."

"It's all right." Zhang rubbed the knuckles of her left hand to comfort her. Her sheepskin robe hung loosely from her neck, the twin swells of her breasts plainly visible, yet she made no attempt to conceal them. He realized his gaze had lingered too long and quickly lifted his eyes to meet hers. "I won't let anything hurt you."

It was the same promise he'd made Li, and the horrible vision leapt once again to the fore of Zhang's mind. He'd sat there, powerless to do anything as the creatures devoured his friend. *Not real*, he reminded himself. *It didn't happen. It can't happen.*

"I've tried to stop them," Dohna said, then she lifted her right hand, held out a knife for his inspection. "But I can't do it."

Zhang tensed; his eyes widened.

"Dohna...may I see that?" He reached for the dagger with a steady hand, and she yielded it to him without struggle. In fact, she looked relieved to be rid of it. Its blade was jagged, chipped, the hilt carved into a tusked face with a protruding tongue. "What were you planning to do with this?"

"Kill *Trapa-la*," she admitted, her voice calm, emotionless.

"Why would you do such a thing?"

She looked as if she might cry, her moist eyes like mirrors, reflecting the dim glow of the flames. "He told you that their chant pacifies the *mamo*."

"Doesn't it?"

Dohna blinked; drawing wet lines down her face. "It *controls* the mamo."

"What are you saying?" Zhang pulled his hand from beneath hers, grabbed her by the arm and shook. "They sent those things to kill my men?-to kill *me*?"

She leaned against him, her tears moistening his cheek. "It is said that when the lord Buddha was attacked, this chant subdued the *mamo*, forced them to become protectors of dharma. Once, they were powerful agents of chaos and destruction, now....now they destroy only those who threaten the roof of the world."

Dohna turned her face so that her words warmed Zhang's ear.

"They've heard what happened down in Chamdo," she told him, "what the People's Army did to the monks and their monasteries—imprisonment; death. Even the Dalai Lama's gone into hiding, afraid of what will happen if he's captured."

Zhang's nostrils filled with the clean smell of her raven hair. "Monks ask forgiveness for even the smallest insects they step on each day. They couldn't murder-"

"They don't consider it murder. It is permissible to fight back in order to defend oneself, so long as you are never the aggressor." Her lips brushed his earlobe. "Your people started this war. *Trapa-la* and the others are only protecting themselves with the *mamo*, protecting dharma...and in the process, holding us prisoner, you and I."

Zhang said nothing. On the chamber floor, the monks sat in neat rows, heads nodding, lips moving in unison; their words formed an endless, monotonous drone, like bees buzzing around his head. And outside, the *mamo* howled their reply.

Dohna said, "If we can stop the chant, the *mamo* would be free to—"

"To smash right through that door." Zhang nodded at the entrance, at the iron bolt and weathered wood that separated them from the horrors beyond.

"Perhaps. But I ask, if your chains suddenly fell away, and you found yourself free of rank and obligation, able to be anywhere, do *anything*, would you attack the very people who had liberated you?" She shook her head and lifted her hand to his chest, her index finger moving as if to trace around his heart. "No, you would run as far from this place as you could, see the world and all its wonders; *live*. I think it would be the same for the *mamo*."

Would Dohna feel that way, he wondered, if she had seen the things he had seen?

Dohna lifted her head from his shoulder; her eyes locked with his, dark and serious. She said simply, "We have to kill the monks, kill *Trapa-la*."

Zhang glanced down at his hand, at the serrated blade he'd stripped from her, at the carved tongue jutting from its hilt, ready to lap spilt blood. Its metal shimmered in the fire-light, showed him flashes of smiling throats. Zhang had taken many lives-a man who could not kill was useless to the People's Army-but slaying unarmed holy men still made his stomach roll.

Dohna seemed to sense his reluctance.

"You've had the vision," she told him, her voice choked with fresh tears, "If you step outside these walls, the chant will bring the *mamo*. It's the only way."

Zhang studied her a moment, her eyes, her lips and her breasts-wondering what it would be like to lay with her for even a single night, to bathe in her warmth.

"I just want to return to my family," she pleaded. "Is that so wrong?"

"No," he said at last. "There's nothing wrong with that at all." And his mind dredged up long-neglected memories of his own far-off kin. Would they even recognize him if he were to return, this girl from Tibet on his arm? "I promise you, no matter what we decide to do, when I leave this place, you *will* be with me."

Dohna offered him a faint smile, and Zhang could no longer control himself. He leaned in and pressed his lips to hers; expecting her to recoil, to beat at his chest with fisted hands, perhaps even to scream. Instead, she hooked one arm around his shoulder and pulled him to her, breathing heavily as she moved her mouth and tongue against his.

The deafening roar of machine gun fire brought the kiss to an abrupt end. Dohna clapped her hands over her ears; buried her face in Zhang's chest. A bullet clipped the column beside them, bits of stone raining into their hair. Zhang's head whirled around, his eyes questing the shooter; he held up the dagger as if it were a shield.

Li stepped from the darkness, gun held at his waist, his wide eyes aiming out across the chamber. The RPD's barrel breathed fire once more; shells spun through the rounded cylinder of the its belly, empty casings dropping down onto Li's boots as he walked.

Hot rounds streaked over Zhang's head, found homes in the nearest monks. The holy men fell forward; red robes appeared to melt across the rough stone. A few stood and ran; most remained in their trances, sustained the chant until Li cut them down.

For a moment, Zhang sat frozen; watched this massacre unfold in slow motion—as if it were the product of nightmare rather than actual events. Then he ordered himself to get up, stumble to his feet; lunge at Li, and his body obeyed. He pushed the RPD's barrel toward the ceiling; stray bullets struck golden prayer bells on the way up, making them ring like windchimes in the cavernous chamber.

"What have you done?" Zhang shouted into Li's face, trying to be heard above the tune.

"Those *things* were going to get us no matter when we left!" Li screamed back. His eyes were wild, fear pushing him to the outer limits of sanity. "I've *seen* it! The girl's right, we had to kill them all, had to stop the damned chant!"

Zhang looked at Li, and then he looked again at the tangle of bodies spilling red across the floor. Bald heads lolled at odd angles, their vacant eyes staring back at him. Their lips stilled, the chamber slowly settled into eerie silence.

There was nothing to be done now. It was finished.

He turned back to Dohna, saw her stumble to her feet, black tresses swaying as she pulled her robe closed, and Yeshe was there.

The abbot stepped up behind her, mouthing the chant; a long, glittering blade clutched in his hands. He lifted the sword above his head, ready to bring it down and cleave her beautiful face in two.

Zhang glanced down at the dagger in his own hand and hurled it. Dohna saw the blade spin toward her and shrank back, startled. The knife whirled harmlessly over her shoulder and struck Yeshe's chest.

The abbot's grip faltered and his sword dropped to the floor with a loud clang. He stumbled backward; sat down hard, his arm draped across the foot of the gold Buddha, covering it in a red shroud. Yeshe's eyes fell to the sculpted hilt, studied it with great fascination. He nodded, blood bubbling from his lips as he spoke, "To destroy...one's enemy is to...to destroy one's self."

Zhang hurried over to Dohna, his hand cradling her cheek. "Are you hurt?"

"I'm fine," she told him absently, her focus on Yeshe. "I do not fear death," the abbot cried out at the ceiling, and then he managed to lift his head and look at them. "I...I fear the world into which I will now be reborn...the world *you* have created."

And then he breathed his last.

Sadly, despairingly, Zhang rubbed Dohna's shoulder and asked, "Do you have a coat?"

She shook her head. "It has been many years since I was outside these walls."

"Then grab blankets and cover yourself with them. We're leaving this place at first light."

At that, Dohna lifted her eyes once more to the wide, peaceful face of the golden Buddha and grinned.

———

Dawn crept tentatively over the Himalayas, as if it were somehow afraid of what its light might reveal. The storm had moved on, leaving a cloudless blue sky and deep white drifts in its wake. And with each frigid step, Zhang, Dohna, and Li left the snow-buried monastery farther behind them-an icy crypt, home now only to death.

"We should cross over into India," Zhang called out. "Start a new life."

Dohna had a thick blanket wrapped around her. She reached up and her long nails dug into the wool, drew it closed around her face, shut out the wind. "My new life has already begun, thanks to you."

Li brought up the rear, his eyes and firearm moving in chorus, scanning craggy peaks on either side of the passage for movement. "Where would they go?"

"Now that the *mamo* are free of their bonds, they can go anywhere in the world," Dohna told them. Hair spilled out through the opening in her blanket like black streamers, becoming twisted and knotted by the wind.

The gorge narrowed, and Zhang suddenly felt the weight of countless stares upon him. He looked up and saw them there, red eyes; they glared out from the hollows of the rocks, glowing hellishly in the darkness. The shadows moved, crept out into the harsh light of day, their talons clicking and scratching at the ice and stone.

"The *mamo* will cause havoc wherever Man lives," Dohna

told them, and Zhang could hear an odd, impish pleasure in her voice. "Foster war, cultivate famine and pestilence... the *mamo's* powers will have no limit."

"No," Li said, spinning in place, aiming his weapon in every direction. "No. No. No."

The *mamo* continued to emerge, emaciated forms, covered in wild manes of thick, matted hair. They reached out; their pointed claws and teeth shimmered in the sun.

Li screamed, nightmares of being eviscerated in his wide, panicked eyes. He shoved his machine gun barrel into his mouth and pulled the trigger, his head blossoming into crimson fireworks.

Zhang slipped his own firearm off his shoulder, his mournful shrieks consumed by greedy winds. He aimed at the moving walls of the canyon, squeezed the trigger, and produced useless clicks. *Jammed!* Zhang tossed the weapon aside, dropped to his hands and knees, and dug through the snow beside Li's corpse, trying to find his friend's gun before it was too late.

"You need no weapons," Dohna told him. She put her hand on his shoulder, and Zhang could feel her long nails through the thickness of his coat. "They will not harm you."

"How do you know?" Zhang asked, tears frozen to his cheeks.

"I know because you have set them free, and because they are my family."

Zhang Lau stopped; shivered.

"When you walked through the temple door," she continued, her voice changing, becoming gutteral; a tiger's growl, "I knew you were the one to break Buddha's spell, the one to finally free me from my prison."

He willed himself to run, but this time his body refused the order. There was no sanctuary from these demons now, no one left to contain them. Dohna had seen to that.

"I want to thank you," she snarled.

Zhang turned his head slowly; knew what he would find despite all his desperate, futile hopes. Whatever glamour the chant had woven had now all but unraveled. The thing dropped its blanket and smiled back at him, still trying to sprout fangs—a twisted parody of its former self.

"Thank you for bringing me home."

# GOODNIGHT

"Why do people have to die?"

The voice was groggy and choked with tears.

Ira Howard looked at his great-grandson. He sighed heavily and sat down on the end of the bed, adjusting the Spider-Man sheets so that they snugly covered the boy up to his chin. Ira still remembered the scared toddler who had been afraid to see him standing at his bedside. As time went by, however, little Tyler grew accustomed to visits from this old man, and now it was not uncommon to find him lying awake as if it were Santa Claus coming by to tuck him in. But there was no joy tonight. The funeral they'd attended that afternoon had not been the first for either of them, but it was the first that Tyler would have memory of, and Ira could tell the kindling of reality had only now begun to spark beneath his seven-year-old eyes.

*Why do people have to die?*

How was he supposed to answer that one?

Was there even an answer he could give?

Some pessimistic acquaintance had once told Ira, "The

moment a person is born they start to die." He could tell this young child that, tell him the mechanics of it all—that the body just runs until it wears out, that God's got everyone's name and expiration date in some holy ledger somewhere—but that would be far too cruel a thing to do. Children should be able to dream without fear of death. That particular fear should be the exclusive reservation of the old and the infirm. But it just doesn't work that way, does it? Death can take anyone at any time.

Even a little boy's mother.

Becky.

His granddaughter.

It seemed only yesterday that Ira was tucking *her* into bed. She'd been a nurse working second shift at the hospital downtown. Three nights ago, headed home after work, she was in an accident. Becky drove a sporty little Saturn coupe. The drunk who killed her was behind the wheel of a Dodge pickup. They met at an intersection just a mile from Tyler's bed, probably as she was on her way to kiss him goodnight. She had the green, the drunk had the red, and neither stopped till they hit one another.

They said she died instantly.

Ira brushed the hair from Tyler's face; his hand soft and decorated in liver splotches. "Did you know I had a twin brother?" It was not an answer to the question he'd been asked, not yet anyway, but the boy didn't seem to care. He shook his little head, his eyes half-lidded. "Yep," Ira told him. "Identical down to every hair on our heads. This was back in 1932, back when I was about your age."

Tyler's sad, sleepy eyes widened a bit at that. Ira thought his great-grandson looked shocked at the idea of this haggard old specter as a little boy.

"I remember it so well," he went on to say. "Peach and

apple pies cooling in mother's kitchen window...playing hide and seek amid sheets drying on the clothesline in the back-yard...running through our father's corn..."

This last memory clouded the old man's dawning smile.

Whenever he'd been out there in the rows with Isaac, his twin, Ira's imagination would always play tricks on him. Thick leaves hid dark spaces where anything might live. There were times when Ira could hear stirring in the distance and his mind would bring forth the worst nightmares it could conjure. Of course, the sounds they heard were made by unseen animals—maybe even their father or one of his hands working to de-tassel the crop, but they'd been seven-year-old boys. There was no television at that time, and Ira had yet to see his first movie. The only entertainment the family had back then was the radio and the radio plays. He would sit there on his living room floor, staring at this wooden box with the lighted tuning dial, and—if he closed his eyes—the sound would give him everything he needed to make a movie in the darkened theater between his ears. When they played in the corn, Ira and his brother Isaac, the sounds they heard weren't animals or people. Those were the sounds of monsters from the radio plays.

Ira shook his head and stared ruefully at Tyler, resuming his tale.

"We'd hear these scary noises, then turn and hoof it back to father's barn—laughing at who'd been more chicken before leaping into the piled hay. One day, when we went and jumped into that haystack...Isaac...he got hurt."

In Ira's mind, they always ran in slow motion. The sound of their giggling seemed to echo through the air. It was just like a movie—one where the audience knows something the char-acters on screen are ignorant of. In this particular film, the audience knew about the pitchfork in the hay. Ira could almost hear the music building as they went to jump, as Isaac did his dive right onto the skewer.

Tyler rose up on his elbows. "You mean he died."

Ira's frown deepened. He remembered yellow hay stained red, remembered shock and agony shaking hands across Isaac's face. Most of all, he remembered his father crying as he scooped up his son and ran with him back to the house. By the time they reached the front step, Isaac had passed out and Dad was soaked down to his knees in blood.

Ira put a hand to his face, pulled his weathered cheeks down to his chin, then gently pushed Tyler back onto his pillow. "He didn't die right then and there. Not then. But my parents knew, if they didn't get some help, he *would*."

"Daddy says an ambulance came for Mommy. He said the Firepeople tried to save her, but she'd already gone to Heaven."

Ira's smile returned. "That's right, Tyler. See, some people go to Heaven right away and others...well, they stay around a while."

"So your Daddy called an ambulance and they saved your brother 'cause he—"

"Oh, no. See, back then we didn't even have a phone. Back then; Harmony was just a bunch of scattered farms somebody somewheres decided they'd call a town. We only had one doctor—Doc Blake his name was—and he was off visiting family that day. There was a hospital in the next town, though, and Dad went to fetch somebody to help."

"They didn't take your brother with them?" Tyler asked softly.

"No. They were too scared to move him. Besides, doctors came right to the house back then. They came out and gave you an exam right there in your own bed. Except, I noticed they didn't put Isaac in *his* bed. They put him in mine. Mom

had wrapped his gut up good—that's where he was hurt—"
Ira gave Tyler's belly a pat. "—the gut—and she was crying
the whole time. Dad had gone off to get the Doctor and it was
just the three of us in that hot little room. Mom sat down in a
rocking chair next to the bed. Her lips kept moving and I
could tell she was praying. I could tell this was bad. I asked her,
'Is he gonna die?' And she looked shocked that I'd even
thought such a thing. She told me, 'He's gonna be fine, Isaac.
He's gonna be right as rain.'"

"She lied, didn't she? She said he'd be fine and then he
died."

"No. What she said she believed. Even if she had her
doubts, she wouldn't want to scare me. But she also got our
names mixed up."

" 'Cause you were twins."

Ira nodded. "And that gave me an idea. It was a silly idea;
now that I look back on it, but at seven...I thought it was the
best idea ever. See, if Mom thought I was Isaac... and if the
Angel of Death was looking for Isaac...why, I thought I'd fool
Death into thinking Isaac was fine. I thought, if Death came
for him, I'd show him my belly and he'd go away. And then
Isaac wouldn't have to die."

Tyler offered his great-grandfather a skeptical look. At
seven, he'd already begun to question things adults told him.
"This is a Fairy story," the look said. "This isn't real at all."

"You believe in angels, don't you?" Ira asked.

The boy looked suddenly hurt. "Sure. Mommy's with them
right now."

"That's right." He squeezed Tyler's shoulder and went on.
"Anyway, like I said, it was a silly idea, but I went with it. That
night, we waited for Dad to come—waited for the Doctor, but
they never showed. It got dark outside and Mom kept wiping
Isaac's sweaty face with a towel. I pretended to be asleep,

pretended not to see her crying and praying. After several hours, holding Isaac's hand in hers, sleep just overcame her. When I think back on it, I think the Angel of Death put her to sleep—made it so she wouldn't see what was gonna happen."

Tyler swallowed. "What happened?"

"After a few minutes, the room got real cold and I see this shadow in the doorway. At first I thought it was Dad, thought he had trouble finding help and he was back to watch his boy die. Then the shadow moved into the room and I realized it wasn't a shadow at all. It was a figure... dressed all in black...Black robe...Black hood...Black wings..."

"It had wings?"

Ira nodded. "Just like an angel, 'cept these were all black—like a raven. He came into the room and walked right over to the end of my bunk—the one where they'd put Isaac. He reached out and grabbed hold of the wooden footboard, and I could see his hands. They were white as ash and you could see each and every bone in his fingers. It was like there was no muscle at all, just skin over bones. The worse thing, though, was the fingernails. They were like bits of that harvest candy corn you like so much 'round Halloween—yellow at the tip and black where they went under the skin."

"Then what happened?"

"I sat up in bed and I says, 'You're here for me, aren'tcha?'"

"Death turned to look at me and I shuddered. I could see a face now, swimming in the dark under that hood. It was a withered face—the face of a man who'd never had so much as a crumb to eat, and it was albino white. There were two holes in his head where his eyes should've been." Ira pointed at his own eyes for emphasis. "Like caves."

"Were you scared?"

"I was so scared, I thought I might just go and wet my brother's bed. But I didn't."

"What did the angel do?"

"Well, he actually walked over to me, and I could smell him way before he got there. Like fruit that's gone bad and drawn flies. He walked over to me, looked me up and down, then he says, 'I was sent for Isaac.' So I tell him, 'I *am* Isaac. But, I'm fine, see.' And I pulled up my shirt to show him my clean, tanned stomach."

"Did he believe you?"

"No. Told you it was a silly idea. The angel knew who he'd come after, and he knew I wasn't it. He just turned around and took a step back toward Isaac."

Ira remembered what happened next all too vividly, but he didn't think he should share it with his great-grandson. Even now, after the eighty years that followed, he still didn't like to dwell on it.

Death had turned around, had taken a step toward his dying brother.

Ira reached out to stop him, clutching a fistful of the specter's cloak (it felt rough, like frayed rope) and a glut of imagery doused his brain. He saw the sons of Egypt crying out in the night...witnessed children covered in black welts, lying on streets of cobblestone...spied men through a wall of barbed wire—yellow stars on their striped shirts and numbers on their arms...beheld a light brighter than the sun and watched it burn a little Asian boy to a cinder...watched helpless as a soldier put a gun to a man's head and fired it...saw a woman bleeding from her eyes beneath a shroud of mosquito netting...witnessed two tall towers crumbling into clouds of debris...saw the end of days. Ira fell back against his pillow; releasing his grip on the garment, and the tour of mortality came to an abrupt halt.

Death glanced back over his shoulder. His face was no longer the malnourished visage of an old man. It was a fanged skull with bonfires blazing in the pitted, hollow sockets of its eyes.

Ira covered his face with his hands. He thought if he looked into those flames he might just turn to salt—the way Lot's wife had on the mountain. God told her not to look at His wrath, not to watch the Angel of Death at work, but she went and did it anyway. He could just see his mother waking up the next morning with one son dead in his bunk and the other a statue. If that happened, he thought the angel might have to come back tomorrow night for her.

"What did Death do?" Tyler wanted to know.

Ira rubbed his eyes. "I screamed at him, 'It's not fair!' Part of my brain was telling me to be quiet, that I might wake up Mom, that Death might do something to her. But I couldn't stop. I *wouldn't* stop. I just kept screaming, 'It's not fair! It's not fair!' Just like you've been screaming it these last three days."

Tyler said nothing, but his eyes could not hide their surprise. He'd been shrieking out at the injustice of it all, but he didn't think anyone knew about that. He'd done it in the silence of his mind, crying himself to sleep at night.

"I told the angel, 'Why was he even born if you just have to go and take him now?'" Ira wiped a racing tear from his great-grandson's cheek. "Wanna know what he said?"

The boy nodded.

"He says, 'He was here so that you would know him, so that your life would be all the better for the experience, so that you could carry his memory with you as long as you might live.' Well, I don't mind saying I thought that was a mighty poor excuse. I didn't want my brother's memory. I wanted *him*."

Tyler nodded his agreement.

"But then Death said something else, he says, 'He will

never leave you. He will watch over you. And you *will* meet again.'"

Upon hearing that, Ira remembered opening his eyes—seeing that Death had returned to his kinder, gentler appearance. He watched the hooded figure bend down and stroke his brother's hair with those spindly fingers. The action was tender and loving, but it made Ira's stomach roll just the same.

"And then the angel grabbed hold of Isaac's hand," he wanted Tyler to know, "and the boy just kind of sat up out of himself. He was still lying there on the bed, still holding Mom's hand, but he was also getting up to stand next to the bunk, holding Death's bony fingers in his own. And you know what? He was smiling. That's what's always stuck with me. My brother was holding this horrid, skeleton hand...and he looked happy about it."

"Did you get to say anything to him? Did you get to tell him you loved him?"

"No, Tyler. I couldn't have said sh—poop if my mouth had been full of it. Besides, he knew all that. All I could do was sit there, watching him. And he just kept smiling, and then he looks over at me and he says, 'Goodnight.' Not, 'Good-bye.' He just said, 'Goodnight.' You know the difference?"

"I think so." Tyler rubbed his eyes, losing his fight against the coming sleep. "Then what?"

"Then the angel spread his black wings and I was out like a light. The next morning, Dad and Mom were crying. They told me Dad's car had broken down, said he had to walk all the way to the next town. By the time the doctor drove him back it was too late. Isaac died."

"Did you tell 'em what you saw?"

"No. Not then. They were too upset. I told my Mom years later, though. She thought it was a dream I must've had."

"But it wasn't."

Ira thought of all the images he'd seen upon touching Death's robe—images of doom both past and future. He saw them again over the years that followed; saw them as they actually occurred. They were all too real.

"No," he said. "It wasn't."

"And your brother watched over you, like Death said he would?"

There were so many times in Ira's life when he felt a presence. When he graduated from high school. On his wedding day. When Becky's father, Richard, had been born. So many times he knew Isaac was with him.

Ira nodded.

"And did you really meet him again?"

The old man smiled. "Yeah. I did."

Tyler yawned, and then—for the first time in days-he too was able to form a grin. Slowly, his eyes fluttered closed and sleep finally wrestled him to unconsciousness.

Ira ran his hand through the boy's hair one last time. He didn't want to leave, but he knew it was time. He wanted to be there to greet Becky, wanted to tell her that her son would be just fine—that Tyler knew she would always be with him. He leaned down, placed a gentle kiss on his great-grandson's forehead, then rose to his feet.

"Goodnight," he whispered.

Ira Howard turned, walked through the wall of the boy's bedroom, and evaporated into the night.

# NOTES

Consider this your "spoiler alert." I'm about to talk about the stories featured in this collection and how they came to be. In some cases, I'm going to let details slip that might ruin the endings and thereby rob you of your ability to enjoy these stories to their fullest. So, if you're a faithful reader who has touched every page of this volume, please, by all means, read on. But, if you're one of those anxious people who like to skip ahead, well...you've been warned.

---

*Jiki*

This story was inspired by my love of Asian horror, the films of Takashi Miike in particular (*Ichi the Killer, Audition*). Much of Miike's early work deals with Yakuza codes of honor and tests of loyalty. One day, as I was doing research into Japanese folklore, I came upon the *Jikininki*-demons who eat the dead-and I thought, "That would be a unique way for the mob to get rid of bodies. A thousand times better than cement shoes!"

After I stopped laughing, the started hammering away on my keyboard.

In an early ending, Jiki came right out and told the dying Koji, "I'm not Emiko." One of my pre-readers, David Lichty, urged me to remove this line. I was reluctant at first, but I do think the story works much better without it.

"Jiki" first appeared in *City Slab* magazine. And, when I opened my contributor's copy, I found my tale right next to an interview with...Japanese director Takashi Miike. Amazing how things work out.

---

*The Bridge*

"The Bridge" was written as the prologue to a novel. I cut it early on due to pacing issues, deciding it was better to let Kim relay this story to a friend in her own words rather than watch it as it happens. In this way, the reader can see how the event still haunts her, and can question whether or not they really believe it took place.

Despite its removal from the manuscript, I loved the tension in this scene, the creepiness of it. It had the feeling of a great campfire tale. And, when *Wicked Karnival* magazine put out a call for Halloween-themed stories, I sold it to them.

---

*Dogs of War*

I wrote "Dogs of War" in the first person...and it just didn't work. Readers immediately suspected that the narrator was crazy. But when I changed it to third person, it had just the opposite effect-they didn't get that he was crazy at all. Then an editor suggested adding the newscaster at the end and it all came together.

When I wrote the final line about the kids, I have to admit, I got goosebumps.

---

*Trolling*

As with so many of my tales, the ending of "Trolling" came to me in a dream. Most people have sex dreams about movie stars, musicians, etc., but mine get directed by H.P. Lovecraft. I wrote it up for a market called, appropriately enough, *Cthulhu Sex*, but the magazine folded. Finally, it saw print in the Indiana Horror Writers anthology, *Dark Harvest*.

---

*Einstein's Slingshot*

I've always been fascinated by dinosaurs. I regularly watch Discovery Channel specials and read news reports on paleontologist's new discoveries. One day, I found a gallery of artwork-paintings of feathered dinosaurs, and I was inspired to write about them.

When I'd finished, I sent the story to *APEX: Science Fiction and Horror Digest*. Editor Jason Sizemore liked the tale, but ultimately rejected it because he said it made him think of *Jurassic Park*. Of course, it was hard for me to be angry; in his letter, Jason compared my writing to O'Henry.

As you might have guessed, I'm a huge *Twilight Zone* fanatic, so the ending was a tip of the hat to Rod Serling.

I hope the master would approve.

---

*God Like Me*

"God Like Me" was my first short fiction sale, so it holds a special place in my heart. The title just popped into my head one day, and I had to come up with a story to fit it. I must confess...I had a fun time writing it. Maybe too much fun. It's probably for the best that I don't possess any psychic abilities.

---

*To Know How to See*

"To Know How to See" holds the record for most re-writes.

This tale was initially set in a high school. I finished my first draft, sent it off to my pre-readers, and then, the very next day...Columbine happened. No editor was going to buy a story about a student who goes on a killing spree in his school cafeteria.

I shoved it into a drawer, but I never forgot about it. I would take the manuscript out from time to time and toy around with it, trying to find a way to make it more marketable (At one point, I even changed the main character's name to Calvin and wrote it as if the kid from *Calvin and Hobbes* had grown up and finally lost all touch with reality). Then, one day it hit me. I simply changed the setting to a spaceship in a distant corner of the galaxy and turned real-world horror into science fiction thriller.

Still wanting to break into *APEX*, I sent the re-write to Jason Sizemore, who wanted me to make it more ambiguous.

He felt, and quite rightly so, that the existence (or non-existence) of aliens should be left up to the reader. This necessitated draft after draft to get the proper mix-add or subtract one detail and it made it too obvious either way. But Jason was patient, and the final result was one of the most satisfying of my career.

---

*For Her*

This was written for a horror anthology that never happened-one where every story had to feature a prostitute. I'd been interested in the *Cihuacoatl* mythos for some time, and, in my twisted little brain, I saw a way to put it to good use here. Having never been to a legal brothel myself, I had to have several lengthy conversations with a lovely lady who worked at a Nevada ranch. Oh, the sacrifices we make for our craft!

When the anthology fell apart, I thought "For Her" would be lost as the market flooded with orphaned prostitute stories. I was pleasantly surprised, however, when it found a home with Tim Deal and *Shroud* magazine. Something about that first line got his attention.

---

*Sanctuary*

I'd always wanted to write about Tibet. I'd researched the clothing, the architecture, the food...but I had no *story*. Then, the opening of this tale played out in my head like a movie—the blowing snow, the glowing eyes, the *fear*. At first, I imagined the creatures as a pack of Yeti, but then I wanted something more original, a creature people might not be as familiar with.

That's when I happened upon the legend of the *Mamo*, and the story almost wrote itself.

---

*Goodnight*

I'd had the idea of twins trying to fool Death for some time, but I didn't really know what to do with it until I had children of my own. One night, while reading my sons a goodnight story, I had this image of my late grandmother West reading to them instead. She died long before they were born, and I wondered what she would think of them, what advice she would give to them if they asked. I tried to write the ideas out as separate stories, but then my muse slapped me upside the head and told me they were two halves of the same tale.

When I finished "Goodnight," I showed it to my living grandmother (something I'd written that I thought she might be able to stomach). She read it in one sitting, then told me that her childhood neighbor died when he jumped into a haystack and landed on a pitchfork. She said she didn't remember ever telling me that, and I didn't remember ever hearing it.

I like "Goodnight" a lot, and it thrills me that the story strikes a chord with so many. It was named the Best Horror Short Story of 2005 in the annual P&E Readers Poll, and people still come up to me and tell me they've read it to their own children. One day, I hope to read it to my children's children.

---

And that's all there is to say. I hope you've enjoyed our time together; I know I have. Now, if you'll forgive me, I hate to be a bad host, but I need to get back to work. There are more stories to write, more tales to tell, and I can't wait to share them with you.

Until next time...
Michael West
Indianapolis, Indiana
June, 2009

# ACKNOWLEDGMENTS

Thanks to: my family, for their understanding, their patience, and their encouragement; Tony Acree and the entire staff at Hydra Publications; Bob Freeman for his amazing artwork; Gary A. Braunbeck for his time, his incredible generosity, and, most of all, his friendship; my army of pre-readers: Dione Ashwill, Jerry Gordon, Sara Larson, David Lichty, Marc Morriston, Natalie Phillips, Brenda Taggart, Ryan Tungate, Chris Vygmont, and Nora Withrow; all the Indiana Horror Writers; and, of course, my faithful readers everywhere.

And thanks to the following individuals for their guidance and their support, both personally and professionally: Julie Astrike, Ericka Barker, Louise Bohmer, Maurice Broaddus, Tim Deal, Kelli Dunlap, Fran Friel, David Garrett, J.F. Gonzalez, Bill Hardy, Kyle Johnson, Brian Keene, Michael Knost, Alethea Kontis, Debbie Kuhn, Michael Laimo, Tom Moran, Rex

Scott, Katrina Shobe, Jason Sizemore, Lucy Snyder, Scott Standridge, Douglas F. Warrick, Wrath James White, and Brian Yount.

# ABOUT THE AUTHOR

Michael West is the bestselling author of Cinema of Shadows, Spook House, The Wide Game, Skull Full of Kisses, and the critically-acclaimed Legacy of the Gods series. He lives and works in the Indianapolis area with his wife, their two children, and their dog, King Seesar.

His children are convinced that spirits move through the woods near their home.

# ALSO BY MICHAEL WEST

The Wide Game

Cinema of Shadows

Spook House

The Legacy of the Gods Book One: Poseidon's Children

The Legacy of the Gods Book Two: Hades' Disciples

The Legacy of the Gods Book Three: Zues' Warriors